Starblazers

Starblazers

by Scott Bredschneider

Editor
Kurt Conrad

Senior Publisher
Steven Lawrence Hill Sr.

Awarded Publishing House
ASA Publishing Company

ASA Publishing Company
Nominated For 2012,2013 BBB Torch Award
105 E. Front St., Suite. 101, Monroe, Michigan 48161
www.asapublishingcompany.com

Copyrights©2013 Scott Bredscheider, All Rights Reserved
Book: Starblazers
Date Published: 01.30.2014
Edition: 1 *Trade Paperback*
Book ASAPCID: 2380634
ISBN: 978-1-886528-73-4
Library of Congress Cataloging-in-Publication Data

This book was published in the United States of America.
State of Michigan

A Publisher Trademark Title page

Table of Contents

Starblazers

by Scott Bredschneider

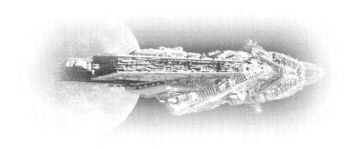

CHAPTER ONE

Initiation

The sun rose over the planet Venus. Humans had pushed out to the stars 1,000 years ago. They had populated hundreds of planets. Since the invention of the jump engines space travel had almost become routine. Connway had read a paper on Jump engines once. In layman terms scientists had figured out a way to sort of fold space like a piece of paper. They could bring the ends of the paper close together, then punch a hole through the two of them and travel through the hole from one point on the paper to the other point, thereby avoiding traveling the entire distance of the paper. The only snag was that the two holes in the paper were not perfectly aligned. It would still take a week's time to enter through the first hole and then travel through slipstream in order to get lined up with the second hole. Still, although this was not perfect it did save years of travel time through normal space. The average citizen usually got to go up at least once or twice in their lifetime. If you happened to work for one of the starship manufactures you may end up in space several dozen times. Connway was a computer tech. He had been born on Venus 31 years ago and he still had not been in space. There were worlds out there with heavy gravity, worlds with ancient underground volcanic tunnels, and even a world that was made of pure water. Connway had read about the water world. Apparently it was possible to take a submarine to the exact center of the planet and you would be completely weightless, just like if you were in space. He was good at his job, or so he thought.

Somewhere in high orbit above the planet a hacker was sitting at a terminal aboard a stolen starship she was reveling in her accomplishment. She had just gotten a guy fired from his job. This was no random firing. She had taken great care to select a highly skilled computer repair technician. She had also selected him for the fact that he had no wife, no children, and no direct family ties on the planet.

Connway was wandering around the starport. He was not quite sure why he was there. "A corporate downsizing," they said. It didn't matter what they called it, he was still unemployed. I mean what was a middle-aged computer tech supposed to do. All the big corporations were hiring all the younger talent. Still, Connway loved his job. As he gazed out an observation window he observed all the spaceships coming and going. The planet Venus had an ammonia-based atmosphere; which is why all the cities were in domes. He watched as one ship came though the massive airlocks that were the gateway to the city. Only medium sized vessels could enter the city.

Larger ships tended to stay in orbit, as they were just plain too big to land.

Connway wandered into a spaceport bar and ordered a drink," A Venution head slammer!"

The bartender looked up and said, "That is a pretty strong drink for a little fellow such as yourself mister."

Connway shot back at the bartender, "Look buddy, I just got fired. Now are you going to get me drunk or not?" The bartender put on his rubber gloves and started making the drink. As he gently set the man's drink on the bar, he slowly backed away and left the customer to himself. Connway sat drinking his sorrows away. He glanced up at the vid screen in the corner of the bar. A local newscast was playing.

The newscast was showing some footage that they had taken in outer space. The information bar at the bottom of the vid screen said that the images had been recorded earlier that morning. The footage showed a starship heavily engaged in a fierce battle. The newscaster proceeded to announce that because the news ship was in a low orbit and the battle was happening in a higher orbit that the news ship could not get a camera angel to see the second ship. However, based on the silhouette of the two ships the announcer said that the light blue colored ship had attacked a vessel nearly twice their own size.

Connway took another sip of his Venution head slammer. Oh yea! It was definitely starting to take effect. As Connway looked back at the vid screen a different newscaster came on saying that they now have a current update to this morning's footage. The cameras then cut from the newsroom to their reporter in the field. As the cameras focused, a beautiful woman with short jet black hair came into view. Behind her in the distance was a light blue colored starship. Holding her microphone the field reporter boldly says, "This is Sarah Odel reporting live from the Nebula Spaceport. As you can see behind me is the infamous pirate ship the *Starblazer*. The Starblazer has again pulled into port for repairs. Little is known about the Starblazers, except that they are known to be some of the most vicious and brazen pirates in the sector. Furthermore nobody seems to know where or what happens to the spoils that the pirates have claimed. The facts are that the Starblazer's ship is believed to be a police grade patrol craft that has been heavily modified as a pure attack vessel. We now go back to our newsroom with a special guest from Ravonloft Industries. Back to you Jim." The news cameras cut back to the newsroom where reporter Jim sits with his expert guest speaker.

Jim says, "Thank you Sarah. I am here in the studio with an engineer from a starship manufacturer. Sir, what can you tell us about the Starblazer?"

"Well Jim," the man proceeds, "as you know we have only been able to examine the Starblazer from a distance. However based on her speed and firepower we know that the ship cannot possibly have any cargo space aboard. You see, it takes very powerful engines to move a medium size vessel that fast. In addition when you take a look at the weapons mounted in the forward turrets you can tell that they are heavy guns. As a matter of fact those guns are far too big to be mounted on a craft that size I would like to take this opportunity to tell all your viewers that Ravenloft Corporation is offering a reward for anyone who can get them the blueprints to the design they are using. That also includes any crewmember of the Starblazer. No questions asked."

Jim laughs saying, "Sir the last time one of our own news ships got to close to the Starblazer they took a pot shot at us. I don't think you are going to get those blueprints anytime soon. Now I would like to introduce our second guest speaker our very own Chief of Police."

"Officer Paul, what can you tell us about the Starblazer?"

"Well um, the Starblazer is a patrol craft vessel that masses 600 tons. Coincidentally, about 3½ years ago a police patrol ship was baited outside the planetary orbital boundary of 500 miles. As you know, once you are over 500 miles outside our planet's atmosphere you are considered to be in open space. The Patrol Cruiser was then ambushed by 4 small ships and never heard from again."

Connway took a hover cab home. He sat on his couch reflecting upon the day, and regretting that Venution head slammer he drank. He decided he should probably go to bed now. Upon standing up Connway suddenly remembered why they called it a head slammer. As the blackness closed in around him he could no longer feel his legs, and he saw the floor rushing up to greet him as he slammed his head on the floor………

Sgt. Tiberious sat at his desk aboard the Starblazer. He picked up his mission file. Inside, it had a picture and personal data of some computer tech. The file was clearly marked 'Disable!' The Sgt. was not sure why an insignificant little tech got the attention on the Starblazers, but then he was not here to question orders. The Captain wants this guy taken out of the game and he was going to see to it that this guy went down. Sgt. Tiberious checked out one of the Starblazer vehicles. A most non-descript hover car that they used when they preferred not to be identified. According to the file the tech worked at some big company named Ravenloft Industries. His target should be easy to acquire leaving work. That evening there was a hit and run accident. Some poor little tech had gotten a broken leg. As the Sgt. Parked the hover car back on board the Starblazer he ordered one of his men to clean the blood off the front bumper.

Connway awoke the next morning. His head throbbing, he wondered why his alarm clock was turned sideways. Then he wondered why his entire living room was turned sideways. Slowly he realized that he was turned sideways! Upon attempting to stand up, Connway felt it was best to remain on the floor. He slowly crawled his way over to the bathroom. He was praying that he still had some oxy tablets to alleviate his hangover. Grabbing onto the sink for stability he managed to get the bottle from the medicine cabinet. The Cap said something about "Push down and twist off," but Connway found it much easier to open if you throw it on the floor and stomp on it!

Sgt. Tiberious received another set of orders. This time he was to hire another crewmember. This was not unusual, since the Starblazer often lost soldiers in combat. However this particular set of orders said he was to locate and recruit a computer technician. Now things were beginning to make sense to the Sgt. Take out one computer geek and replace him with one that would be loyal to us! Ah! Yes, subterfuge was one of his favorite games.

It was midafternoon now and Connway was feeling much better. He figured it was time he started looking for a new job. He glanced down at his left arm. He was still wearing the forearm computer that he used for work. It belonged to the company, but apparently they forgot to ask for it back. It was a rather expensive piece of equipment. But hey! If they don't ask, he was not going to tell them he still had it. Coincidentally, or maybe not so, his videophone rang. Upon answering Connway was greeted by a rugged looking man wearing a spiffy black suit and tie. The man proceeded to greet him. "Good morning Mr. Connway, we heard that you were recently unemployed. Well it just so happens that my company is looking to hire a talented computer tech just such as yourself. Why don't you meet me for an interview in one hour?"

Connway could not believe his luck; he hadn't even started looking for a job yet. When he arrived at the restaurant he sat in a corner booth sipping water this time. While he waited, he heard the front door of the restaurant fly open and people getting out of the way. Upon looking to what the commotion was he was horrified to see four men in light blue Starblazer uniforms. Connway thought to himself, "Oh no, this could ruin my interview!" Just then the four men fanned out revealing a fifth man. This was the rugged looking man who fixed his eyes directly on Connway. Connway froze in his tracks. It was his interviewer!

Sgt. Tiberious shouted, "There he is men. Grab him!" As the four soldiers hefted Connway to his feet they hauled him outside and shoved him into an armored tactical hover jeep. Sgt. Tiberious sat in the jeep across from Connway and stretched out his hand. "Congratulations Mr. Connway, you have managed to make it this far without getting yourself killed."

Connway nervously reached out to shake the man's hand. With only a slight quiver in his voice Connway managed to ask, "Where are you taking me?"

Sgt. Tiberious just grinned and said, "To see the Captain."

As the tactical hover jeep pulled into the starport, Connway looked out the window to see an impressive looking light blue colored ship. On the side of the ship was a painted skull atop a pair of crossed lightning bolts with the logo Starblazers emblazoned across its hull. Connway never expected in a million years to ever be this close to a pirate ship. Especially the Starblazer! And now he was going aboard to meet the Captain.

A S A   P u b l i s h i n g   C o m p a n y

CHAPTER TWO

The Job

As Connway entered the bridge under heavy escort he was surprised to see that the lights were kept very dim. He could just make out a figure sitting in a command chair in the center of the room. The voice informed him that the Starblazers are preparing to make their next big move.

As the Captain spoke a disguised voice said, "First let me fill you in on some background information that is not widely disseminated to the general public. You see whenever countries, or sometimes entire planets go to war they tend to take the fight into outer space. That way the very land, which they are fighting over, does not get obliterated in the battle. Regardless of who wins the battle there is always a debris field left floating in space full of smashed warships. Normal procedure is for the victor of the battle to go back and salvage the wrecked starships. However I have decided that it is time for the Starblazers to acquire a larger ship."

The Captain reaches down by a holster and comes up brandishing a laser pistol. As the Captain points it directly at Connway, the Captain asks, "So Mr. Connway, this damaged vessel that we are going to steal is going to need some repairs made to her computer core. Do you think you can assist us?"

Connway was paralyzed with fear. He wanted to run but his feet would not move. Trying to control his speech while the laser gun was pointed at his forehead he said, "Uhm … sure."

The Captain replaced the laser gun back in its holster and said, "Wonderful! I like the way you handle yourself with confidence. You know the last tech we offered this job to was quaking with fear and tried to run out on me. We had to shoot him."

On their way to Connway's quarters aboard the ship, Sgt. Tiberious explained to Connway that special arrangements had been made for him to be the replacement for a computer tech who recently broke his leg in a terrible hover car accident. Connway's instructions are to go with a salvage team to recover a large ship from the debris field of a battle site. There would be three other members on the salvage team. An environmental systems expert, a pilot and propulsions engineer. His job of course is to repair the computer core. Once the ship has enough power and ability to move the salvage team is supposed to fly it to Ravenloft Industries, "But we want you to change the jump coordinates and bring it to us. The salvage team of course is expendable once they have completed their respective assignments."

As Connway entered his quarters, he found both regular clothes, a Starblazers uniform and a set of Ravenloft salvage crew overalls laid out for him. As he put on the overalls he noticed everything was in his correct size. He wondered how the Starblazers knew so much about him. This also bothered him just a little bit! As he looked through the room he also found a data pad. Curious as to why it was with the tool belt for the overalls he checked the file directories. There was one file in particular labeled 'Transmit'. As data pads do not normally do much of anything he investigated it more thoroughly. Sure enough, there was an imbedded signal transponder hidden in the unit's circuitry. Clever, he thought. Only a trained computer technician would have the skills to locate and detect the device and that was him. If he got in any trouble he could use this signal for help. Connway paused for a moment; he could not believe that he was about to go off with pirates to steal a warship. Still he had nothing better to do, and he did not really want to upset the pirates. So he grabbed his gear and one of the crew gave him a ride over to Ravenloft Industries.

Ravenloft Industries was amongst the biggest starship manufacturers on the planet. They even had space dock facilities for building the larger ships in orbit. The entrance lobby alone was impressive. There were marble floors with fluted columns that reached up three floors. Floating in the middle of the entrance was a static 3-D holographic image of the company's logo. A Raven perched high atop a mountainside.

Sgt. Tiberious reported to the Captain that they were ready for liftoff. As the Starblazer crafts engines powered up, and the navigator obtained flight clearance from the tower, the Sgt. could feel the power in the deck plates of the ship. The Starblazer had to restrain itself to one-quarter speed while within the planet's atmosphere. Otherwise the speed would create so much air friction that it would overheat the hulls surface. Friction burn was not normally a worry for most ships. But then again, most ships did not have the powerful engines they had. The Sgt. let out a little smile of satisfaction.

Connway's arrival at Ravenloft Industries completed the assembly of the salvage team. Introductions were made. First there was Philip, the engineer. Philip was an older gentleman who had spent nearly 19 years working for Ravenloft. He was considering retiring, but wanted to take this one last opportunity to go into deep space just for fun. A man named Jacks was the pilot. Jacks also worked for Ravenloft. He was a former "Space Marine" and his assignment was to fly the recovered ship home. The third crewmember was Michele, the environmental systems analyst. Connway could not help but notice her lovely jet-black hair and striking resemblance she had to that reporter on TV. Sarah Odel. Connway wondered if they were related. Finally, there was Connway himself. He decided to introduce himself as the computer repairman; as opposed to a Starblazer pirate here to steal the vessel.

The salvage team was given a small recovery ship that massed 100 tons. After passing through the security scanners he climbed aboard. Connway could not help but feel a little cramped in the comparatively smaller ship, with no weapons. The Starblazer was a much larger craft and heavily gunned. Of course all those upgrades made the Starblazer cramped as well, but at least crew quarters were still fairly roomy. The salvage vessel was not due to lift off for another 4 hours, so Connway decided to use his time productively. He hacked his way into Ravenloft's computer system and got some information on his crewmates. Personnel files were restricted access. So Connway did an end run and downloaded all information pertaining to the current salvage operation. Connway chuckled to himself, "If you can't unlock the front door, open the garage door!"

"So, where to start now," he thought. All right, the engineer could shut down the engines and jeopardize him delivering the vessel to the pirates. Philip's personnel file told him that the engineer's father and grandfather before him all worked in the propulsion field. They worked on and off for Ravenloft Industries at various times. Philip's managed to get a full time job with Ravenloft and appeared to love his work. It seemed that Philip had even passed up a promotion one time because the job would have put him at a desk, and Philip apparently liked working with his hands and getting a little grease on his face.

Next was Jacks, the pilot. He was a dedicated, qualified pilot and navigator. He was qualified with several different weapons and had combat training. Connway definitely did not like the potential problems this man posed, as Connway was going to have to discreetly change the jump coordinates and a trained navigator would definitely notice that.

Finally there was Michele, the environmental systems analyst. Wait a minute ... that was Michele Odel. Connway thought she looked familiar. She was the sister of that reporter. Connway was not entirely sure what to make of this. But then he still needed her to fix the ship. Also in her file was the fact that she was an outside contract. She apparently did not work for Ravenloft. But there was no mention of what company that she did work for. There were however records of her academic history. Apparently in addition to environmental controls she also took an awful lot of martial arts training. Now what was a beautiful girl like that doing with those skills?

The Starblazer reached an altitude of 100 miles above the planet. Being clear of atmosphere the pilot began to open her up. As the engines spun up, Sgt. Tiberious checked the radar screens. The Starblazer was already moving faster than half the ships currently in orbit. Still even though all of their raids are conducted past the 500 mile mark it was still possible that some of the shipping companies that they have hit in the past might try to get some kind of revenge. He felt that a fast departure was always a prudent move. As he checked the rear viewing cameras, he saw the greenish blue ammonia gasses of Venus swirling below. A feeling of contentment nestled in the Sgt.'s belly.

The salvage team was ready for liftoff. All crew were accounted for. As the ship attained a low orbit the pilot Jacks appeared to panic, "Damn! Pirates." Jacks grabbed the radio and called for the police. He informed them that he had spotted a pirate vessel the Starblazer within the 500 mile orbital border.

Connway looked across the cockpit and informed Jacks that the Starblazers historically have never attacked inside the 500 mile barrier. He was also relatively positive that they were going to be left alone. Jacks shot back saying, "I don't care. I simply don't like pirates." Connway kept quiet, but not without making a mental note about Jacks' dislike for pirates.

Aboard the Starblazer Sgt. Tiberious called out to the Captain, "Radar shows we have a police cruiser moving to intercept." The Captain asked for a range, and time to firing distance?

The Sgt. replied, "200 miles out, 5 minutes Captain."

The Captain laughed, "Ha, he will never close the distance in time. Helm, we have an appointment to keep. Throttle up and let's get out of here."

As the Starblazer pulled away from the sluggishly slow police cruiser the crew began preparing for jump. As they reached the 500 mile orbital mark the Captain gave the order to jump. The entire ship seemed to fold into space, real space doubled back on itself, and the ship began to slip through space. An average jump would take one week regardless of distances involved. Slipstream travel was always a bit eerie, but rather efficient.

As the salvage ship moved into a higher orbit Jacks was relieved to see the Starblazer moving off, and said so too. Connway hardly aware of his own comment, mumbled under his breath, "We have a coward for a pilot." Michele's attention perked up. Jacks may not have heard Connway's comment, but she did. Michele looked Connway up and down. Thinking to herself, 'that is a rather bold statement coming from a computer tech.'

The salvage vessel began its jump procedure. Sliding into the slipstream the crew could now sit back and relax for the next week. The ship was capable of autopilot once they were inside slipstream. Over the course of the next week the crew had a chance to get to know each other on a more personal level. Connway tried to keep his conversations simple, so as not to arouse any suspicion.

Meanwhile he had a hidden agenda. He had to find out whom he could trust and who would cause him problems when he stole the warship. It was already apparent to him that the pilot had to go. Jacks did not like pirates and the moment that Connway changed the jump coordinates he would be detected. Connway just did not know how to eliminate him yet. Conversely, Philip the engineer spent most of his time back by the engines. Connway actually had to go back to the engine room to speak with him. But his efforts turned out to be very lucrative. Although Connway had to sit through several hours of the old man's ramblings on about this propulsion system as compared to that propulsion system and why one drive was better than another drive. In the end Connway learned that this fellow did not care about much else just as long as he got to work on the biggest most powerful engines he could lay his hands on. At the same time it seemed that Philip appreciated the fact that someone had taken an interest in his work. This rapport could possibly be used to Connway's advantage in the future.

Michele on the other hand was a tough nut to crack. She was pleasant to speak with but there were several gaps in her life story. She was in fact sister to Sarah Odel the reporter, but at the same time she did not seem to be very close to her. Connway also discovered it was difficult for him to talk with her, as his eyes kept wandering up and down her trim firm body. During the course of the week Connway would occasionally catch a glimpse of Michele working out to stay in shape. She would be wearing tight spandex shorts and glistening with sweat!

Michele would sometimes catch him looking at her out of the corner of her eyes. But she never said anything. She just took a subtle satisfaction in that she still had it and enjoyed the attention.

As far as Connway himself was concerned, whenever a crewmember asked about himself he generally would fall back to his life as a corporate computer junkie. When asked why he was on this particular assignment he simply said that he volunteered, because he wanted to get out more.

The Starblazer dropped out of jump space. She had arrived at the pre-set coordinates. Hanging in deep space were four ships. They massed 100 tons each. The cargo ships reported in that they had sold the captured booty, and had payroll checks ready to distribute to the crew of the Starblazer. After getting paid the crews of the five ships did what every crew normally did after getting paid. They broke out the beer and proceeded to get drunk!

The salvage ship arrived at her destination. Just outside a debris field. Sure enough, there were hundreds of wrecked craft scattered about. Connway had never seen such wreckage before. Jacks began his sensor sweep. He scanned the remains of shattered scout ships, the twisted hulls of fighter craft and the blown out deck of a carrier ship. Finally after about a half hour Jacks announced that he had located their target vessel. Jacks was a bit apprehensive. He informed the others that their target vessel was located in a particularly dense part of the debris field. He further advised everyone to get into their spacesuits as a precaution against a hull puncture from all of the sharp shrapnel floating around outside.

The salvage ship was not a real private place due to the fact that it was such a small vessel. Michele and Connway were both in the air lock putting on their spacesuits. As Michele bent over and slid into her suit she put her hand on Connway's shoulder to steady herself. This would not have been unusual, except when she was done she slid her hand down his back in a lingering type parasol. Connway, feeling a slight closeness, decided to flirt back. He gently brushed up against Michele's leg. As he did so he hit an object in one of the tool pockets on her thigh? It felt very distinctly like a gun. A small hold out gun, but never the less, a gun! Connway's mind was racing. What was she doing with a gun, and how did she get it aboard past the security scanners? Michele acknowledged Connway's flirtatious nudge and just smiled.

Jacks called over the ships intercom that he was taking them into the debris field. The first few minutes went fine. It was the next few minutes that unsettled Connway. There was a very loud clang that rang through the ship as it lurched to one side. Connway was nearly thrown off his feet while Jacks could be heard swearing from the cockpit. Michele said that a large chunk of metal must have just bounced off the starboard side. As Jacks bobbed and weaved through the debris field he narrowly avoided countless collisions with fragmented starships.

Over the intercom Connway heard Philip call forward, "My gauges say the starboard maneuver thruster has been hit!" Jacks responded, "Roger, compensating now!" Just then there was a piercing scream and rending of metal. The port side of the ship brushed up against an exceptionally large and serrated chunk of space wreckage. It tore a small gash in the side of the ship about 4 inches long. They were losing atmosphere fast! Connway was glad he was wearing his spacesuit. Connway was almost knocked over as he saw Michele race past him. She viciously threw open the door to a gear locker and proceeded to ransack it. As the air rushed out of the gash in the hull, it began to suck out small objects into the blackness of space. First it was a stray pen, then a data pad, and now Connway could feel the vacuum pulling at him. Michele emerged from the gear locker with a 12-inch steel plate in her left hand and a spray can in the other. She let go of the plate and it hung in midair. Even though the ships artificial gravity was working fine the plate remained aloft. Then with a sudden tumble and acceleration the plate violently smacked against the inner hull covering the breach. As the edges of the plate hissed Michele quickly lunged forward and emptied the contents of the spray can around the outer rim of the plate. The auto sealing foam took effect almost immediately sealing the breach! Michele triumphantly turned around to see Connway still standing there in awe. Michele cheerfully smiled and said, "Patch kit! Handiest damn things ever invented."

As the air pressure began normalizing in that section of the ship; Jacks announced that they had reached a small clearing in the debris field near their target vessel. Bringing the ship to a stop the salvage crew now had a new challenge to face. The target vessel was dead in space. There were no running lights, or any signs of power. The crew was prepared for this. Still, it would have made their job a lot easier if it still had power.

As Jacks gently engaged the maneuver thrusters the rest of the crew crowded into the cockpit. Looking out the windshield, Jacks slowly circled the target vessel. They could see that the destroyer class ship had obviously fought bravely. There were heavy score marks all along the hull. Horrible plasma burns across the side, and several ruptures. As they circled around to the port side they were stunned to see that the entire port side engine was gone! It had been completely blown out from the inside. Philip moaned. He knew something had to have gone terribly wrong for that engine to have exploded in that manner. Still, the vessel had survived. Philip was confident he could still get enough power out of the starboard engine to get it moving again if he could get it up and running.

Michele was looking for the name of the vessel. She saw the hull markings with the letters "OS****" but the rest of the name was obscured by plasma burns. After the fly by; Jacks and Philip had determined that the best point to enter the 'Os' would be through the cargo bay. Unfortunately the bay doors were closed. Someone would have to go in through a side hatch and open the doors from the inside.

Philip clicked on his magnetic boots. He was used to walking on the outside of starships. After all you sometimes had to make repairs to the hull. Only this time he would have to disengage his boots, leap over to the target vessel, re-engage his boots and carry the emergency power pack all at the same time. Fortunately the target vessel was much larger than the salvage ship. The target ship should be relatively easy to hit. The only thing Philip was worried about would be the sudden stop.

Philip turned on his head set so that he could communicate with Jacks on the bridge. Philip took a deep breath and said, "Well here goes nothing guys!" With a click of his heals he shut off his magnetic boots and gently pushed off. As Philip floated away he got a serious sinking feeling in the pit of his stomach. It kind of reminded him of a roller coaster, only without any safety controls and much deadlier consequences. As Philip drifted toward the dead ship he began to notice that he had a slight rotation. He was not going to land on his feet! Remembering about his feet he clicked his heals together and reactivated his magnetic boots. Philip tried to estimate his rotation. He was going to hit on his back. He still had a moment to think about it. He could deal with this; after all it is only life or death if he screwed up. When Philip hit the dead ship he quickly raised his right knee and planted his foot against the hull with a clank. Next the power pack bounced on the hull, and finally his other foot made its mark. With the inertia still carrying him forward he slowly stood up in the upright position. Philip took a moment to get his bearing and reassure himself, "Yea, I meant to do that!"

The Starblazer and its four cargo ships were beginning to recover from their celebrating. It was time to get back to work. They had an errand to run. As they set coordinates for their jump, Sgt. Tiberious got a shudder down his spine. Their destination was a quarantined planet that they had their base on. The planet had long since cleansed itself of the plague that had killed all its inhabitants. Still, it gave the Sgt. an eerie feeling every time he thought about it. It would take them a week to get through jump space. It was just as well. The Sgt. had some reading to catch up on anyway.

Philip was a little concerned about the power pack banging against the hull of the ship like that. However, he did not really have time to worry about that right now. His spacesuit only had about 2 hours' worth of air. As Philip made his way over to the small airlock door he could see that several laser blasts had impacted that area. He pulled a 'T' handled wrench out from his tool belt and tried to manually open the hatch. It was no use; the door was warped and jammed. Philip quickly searched his tool belt. Pulling out his plasma-cutting torch he plugged it into the power pack. Pausing for one moment he took a labored breath and pushed the button. With a sigh of relief he saw the torch spring to life. The power pack did not get damaged on the trip over. Philip began cutting near one of the laser score marks. He needed to make every inch of his cut count. The plasma torch uses a lot of power and he was going to need that energy to open the bay doors.

The hatch finally nudged open. With a few more turns of the "T" handle Philip had gotten inside. It was a tight fit inside the airlock when he dragged in the power pack. As he closed the hatch he took hold of the cable to the power pack and plugged it into the receptacle on the wall. The air lock instrument panel lit up. Philip smiled thinking, 'Well at least something works on this tub.' He checked the gauges. They were reading that the area of the ship on the inside of the hatch still had air pressure. This was good news. Unfortunately it was also reading red. Toxic levels, the air was contaminated, not breathable. Philip mumbled, "Well that is probably why we brought an environmental systems expert."

As he pushed the button to close the outer hatch and start the air lock sequence the instrument panel was not reading a positive seal on the outer door. Philip's day was just not going right. The warped hatch had to be fixed quickly; he had already used 30 minutes worth of air from his spacesuit. Philip had to think. "Screw it," he thought. He raised his plasma torch and started welding himself in! Upon finishing the last bit of weld he glanced back to the instrument panel. GREEN. He pushed the button and the inner door slid open. Disconnecting his power pack he toted it along behind him. The pack floated nicely along in zero gravity. As his magnetic boots clinked down the corridor he kept his eyes open for another terminal. The lights on his helmet illuminated the dark passageway and glistened off of a reflective surface. It was an instrument panel, he was sure of it.

As Philip approached the glistening object something came into view. It was a dead crewman! His spacesuit torn and a frightfully contorted face displayed the horrors of decompression. Philip cringed. What a tragic way to die. Speaking of dying he reminded himself he had to keep moving, he only had another hour and fifteen minutes of air left in his suit. Pushing past the ghostly figure he proceeded down the hall.

Finally he came upon another terminal. Plugging in the power pack the unit came to life. He quickly called up a floor plan of the star ship. The cargo bay was just around the corner. He could have guessed that much, but what he really wanted was a wiring schematic. Searching through directory after directory he finally found what he was looking for. The junction point to tie into and supply power to the cargo bay doors. He checked the power pack. It was reading just over half power. He was burning too much energy with the plasma torch and these computer terminals. He had to conserve power for the bay doors.

Philip arrived at the cargo bay easily enough. Unfortunately the work lights on his spacesuit only illuminated the first 30 feet. This was a very large bay and the junction box he needed to patch into was on the other side, and on the ceiling. He did not have the time to casually search the bay on foot. He clicked his heals and turned off his magnetic boots. Pushing off into the blackness he drifted across the void at a slight upward angle. As he floated through the bay he felt something brush his thigh. In a near panic he looked down. His spotlight lit up a nut and bolt that was free floating around. He wondered how much other space junk was in here with him. As the opposite wall came into view he reactivated his magnetic boots and raised his foot. He was starting to get the hang of this. As he contacted the wall he steadied himself and began walking. He was now walking up the walls towards the ceiling. His sense of spatial orientation was improving. Glancing around, he found his junction box. After plugging in the power pack he punched up the commands for the cargo bay door. God, he thought. They better open, because if they are jammed, then he is dead!

The crew on the salvage vessel was pleased to see the bay doors open. Jacks maneuvered the salvage vessel into position. The bay doors were sluggish, but moving nonetheless. Philip decided it was time to turn on the lights; he was tired of wandering around in the dark. He reached over and touched a button on the control panel. The bay lights began to glow.

Jacks could see the bay coming to life. The doors were about half way open now.

As Philip looked up, or rather down, from the ceiling he was over swept with concern. The bay was full of space junk! Everything from wrenches to power cables were free floating throughout the bay. Just then the bay lights dimmed and extinguished. The bay doors quit moving. Philip smacked the emergency power pack and screamed, "NO, you piece of junk!" The pack was completely dead.

Outside Jacks had managed to get a glimpse of the bay. When he saw the lights die and the bay doors stop moving he knew there must be a problem. Still the bay doors were half-open. Jacks considered this for a moment and thought about the salvage vessel. The tiny ship was triangular in shape and relatively thin and wide. If he turned sideways relative to the target vessel he may be able to squeeze in. He was a good pilot and this presented him with an interesting maneuver. Firing his maneuver thrusters Jacks re-oriented his vessel. Jacks just barely touched his rear thrusters; the ship began to gently drift forward toward the bay.

Michele was looking over the shoulder of Jacks, her teeth biting the edge of her lip. She had been in some interesting places in her life, but she had to admit this was a new experience. Connway could see the edge of the bay doors getting uncomfortably close to the salvage vessel. Connway left the bridge. Connway reappeared on the bridge a moment later. Michele looked over at him. He was holding a 12-inch steel plate and a can of auto sealing foam. Michele smiled.

Philips checked his spacesuit. He had 20 minutes of air left. Suddenly the cargo bay was illuminated again he looked down to see the salvage vessel had turned on its search lights and was trying to squeeze through the half open doors. He adjusted the radio on his helmet and called to Jacks. "Hey buddy, good to see you. By the way you are a bit high you are about to shear your communications array on top of the ship."

Jacks fired the maneuver thrusters and came down a touch. As he eased her in, there was the audible sound of wrenches and bolts pinking against the hull. A glove from a spacesuit smacked against the windshield of Jacks' cockpit, it slid off to the port side. As they continued forward Connway heard a scraping sound against the hull. Philip called in, "Don't worry about that one, It is just a loose cable; it is not attached at the other end." Jacks extended the landing pads. Michele could see that Jacks was completely concentrating on piloting so she reached over to the control panel and flicked on the magnets. Jacks brought the ship down and contacted the floor. "Touchdown!" he cried.

Philip chuckled and spoke into his radio, "Um … Jacks, you do realize that you are stuck to the side wall right? I mean spatial orientation and all that."

Jacks frowned and replied, "Hey, you want to fly this thing or what?"

Philip looked at his air gauge and said, "Never mind just open the air lock … I am coming back in."

As Philip returned, Michele handed a spool of wire cable to Connway. Connway looked puzzled and asked, "What am I supposed to do with this?"

Michele replied, "That is a comm cable, go outside and plug one end into the external port on the salvage ship and the other into a terminal port of "OS" ship. I need to see what systems are functioning and which ones are not." Connway asked why he had to do it.

Michele put one hand on Connway's shoulder and the other gently on his chest with a warm smile and said, "Pleeeease. After all I am just a girl."

Connway blushed; he put down his patch kit and proceeded out the air lock to hook up the cable. Connway didn't really know what he was doing. This was his first spacewalk, and he was trying to get used to the sensation of zero gravity. He would be happy if Philip got the power up and the gravity generators on the 'OS' back on. As he fumbled around, Michele got on the radio and was giving him tips on how to move about. Connway wondered how come she knew so much, and since she did why was he out here?

Philip came up to the cockpit and could tell by the professional pep talk that Michele was giving Connway that she knew very well how to move around in space and that she was obviously trying to teach Connway. Philip just smiled and left it alone.

The crew had had a pretty full day. The next morning Michele started checking systems via the patch cable Connway had so graciously installed for her. Meanwhile Connway sat wondering why he was outside trying to get used to zero gravity and Michele was giving him tips over the radio when she was supposed to be this innocent young girl who didn't know anything. Oh yea, and what about that gun?

Michele reported that the ship's artificial intelligence computers were down, but that she was able to access environmental controls. She had shunted power from the salvage ship to several isolated systems aboard the 'OS'. The ship had roughly 20% of the compartments still under pressure. Unfortunately, the air was still toxic to breath but she was going to go locate the scrubbers and try to fix that. She put on her spacesuit and set off to explore the 'OS'.

As Michele explored the dead ship she wandered around corner after corner. She knew it was a large ship, but now that she was aboard it seemed absolutely massive. The work lights on her helmet provided sufficient light while she floated along. She actually did not mind that the artificial gravity was not working yet. It made it much faster for her to move along. As she searched for the air purifiers she came down a corridor which had a placard on the wall. There were frozen ice crystals obscuring the lettering. She floated up to it and put out her hand out to stop her forward momentum. As she came to a stop her hand brushed away the ice to reveal the letters 'OS'. As she cleared the rest of the placard she found the name of the ship, 'The Osiris'. Michele tried to remember her history classes. Osiris was an Egyptian god. The gatekeeper of the dead. She thought to herself, 'What an appropriate name for a Destroyer.'

Philip was eager to get to the engine room. The Osiris was a destroyer class ship and he could not wait to get under the hood and lay his hands on her engines!

Jacks figured he would go check out the bridge, and of course Connway was bound for the central computer core.

For the next five days they hardly saw Philip. He was knee deep in engine parts and he had a big silly grin on his face to prove it!

Michele had her hands full with the environmental systems, but was making progress. Jacks, on the other hand, was disappointed. When he got to where the main bridge was he manually cranked open the door and looked directly out into the blackness of space. The bridge had been a casualty of combat. It took him a day and a half to locate the auxiliary bridge. Normally it would have taken him only moments to find, but the computers were not up yet. So he had to resort to a deck-by-deck search.

Connway discovered that the Osiris actually had three separate A.I. computers. This made sense to him since this was a destroyer class ship, and when rolling into battle you had to have a backup system in case you were damaged. Given the fact that these computers were A.I.'s it was common for computer tech's to name them. Since it was going to require him to restart and reboot the computers in order to install himself as the commander and set new security passwords he was also going to have to rename them. He postulated this for a moment and decided he would name them after an ancient TV show that he heard about once. With a proclamation, to no one in particular, he raised his hand and said, "I now proclaim you to be Larry, Mo, and Curly!"

Jacks was busy cleaning the secondary bridge. There were blown out panels and dead crew floating all over the place. Jacks began flushing the dead crewmembers out the airlock. After a while it was starting to look like a command deck again.

Somewhere around day 3 Philip had managed to get the power up, which was rather convenient, as now they all had lights to see with. Jacks was now inputting jump coordinates into the navigation computer. It would not be too long before the Osiris would be ready to limp back to a star port for real repairs.

Connway discovered that the first A.I. (Larry) was done! His components were located on the port side of the ship, which had been severely damaged. He was beyond repair. So he directed is attentions toward 'Mo'. Mo was coming along well. Mo reported that he had 34% of his sensors on line and that he was having a nice day. Connway reminded Mo that he was 66% damaged or blinded. Mo playfully reminded Connway that a week ago he was floating in the coldness of dead space. Unbeknownst to Connway as he worked on repairing some of Mo's memory circuits, Mo began scanning the debris field. The last thing Mo remembered before he was knocked out was being right in the middle of a pitched battle. He wondered who had won.

Mo's memory crystals were foggy. But the longer Connway worked the clearer Mo's mind was getting. Soon, Mo remembered what he was doing. Mo was a destroyer and he was sent to crush the insurrection on the mining planet of Mercury. The underground colonies had been funded and supported by various super corporations; the corporations were not about to allow them to break away. After all, the super corporations had a substantial financial investment to protect.

The Mercurians however knew this. They had spent years secretly building their own private fleet of warships. They had managed to go undetected because the intense solar radiation from being located so close to the sun caused interference and sensors often got clouded. When the Mercurians declared their independence they immediately sent up their defense fleet. The Corporations in turn launched 'I.A.F.', the *Insurrection Abatement Force*.

The battle turned out to be a very hard fought fight, which swung back and forth without a clear winner for a long time. As it turned out the Mercurians had to build their ships with extremely thick hulls in order to stave off intense radiation in their area. Although the Mercurian ships were much smaller than the I.A.F.'s they proved to be quite durable. It took an average of two equally sized I.A.F. ships to bring down one Mercurian vessel of equal mass. The Mercurians however did not have any destroyer class vessels. The Osiris inflicted massive casualties! Mo was an I.A.F. ship, and was never told that the battle was over. He continued to scan for enemy ships.

Mo checked his internal sensors. There was the possibility that he had been boarded by foreign invaders. Upon conducting a search for crew he found four life forms aboard. Mo attempted to verify the life form's identity by checking it against his crew manifest. Unfortunately the crew manifest was contained in a section of memory crystals that had not been repaired yet. Mo scanned to see what the life forms were doing. One of them was working on his systems directly, powering up computer system after system. Mo deemed that this must be a friendly crewmember. The next was a female who appeared to be attempting to restore air pressure to various compartments. She was fixing things as opposed to disabling him. She was deemed as being some type of technician that maintained systems and therefore must be a valued crewmember. A third was in the engine room doing his best to effect repairs. Analysis = friendly. And the fourth was flushing crew out an airlock. Mo believed there was a border attempting to take him over. The problem was he was currently in no condition to fight back.

CHAPTER THREE

The Kill

Connway realized that they would soon be ready to jump the ship back to civilization. He was going to have to do something about Jacks. They were all now able to move about the undamaged portions of the ship. Since Michele had detoxed the air. Connway asked Mo for the location of Jack?

Mo replied, "Who?"

Connway forgot that the salvage crew was not part of the original Osiris crew. Connway rephrased his question to "What is the location of the other humans aboard the Osiris?"

Mo said that his internal sensors detected four humans on board at this time.

"Okay," Connway retorted, "One of them is a girl and one of them is me. Now where are the other two?"

Mo answered, "One is in my engine room and the other on the secondary Command Bridge."

Connway had never even considered killing anyone before. But then again if he did not deliver the ship to the Starblazers he was sure that they would kill him. He began to form a plan. He would need a spacesuit and some tether line.

He would also need the help of one of the A.I.'s. Although he was doing nicely with Mo, he also remembered that he had read somewhere that an A.I. can become psychologically unstable just like a real human.

Mo had already gone through the trauma of Battle, freezing space, and reactivation in a reduced capacity. Connway did not want to stress him out any further by asking him to help kill another human. On the other hand this was a combat ship and the computers had certain laws of robotics removed in order to enable them to target and fire on other vessels.

Connway went to speak with Mo. He asked Mo if he had any ethical problems with assisting in the execution of Jacks.

Mo responded, "I do not have him on my registry as part of the Osiris crew. I would be happy to purge this invader from my bowels." Connway was taken aback by the callous attitude Mo had about the mere purging of life.

Connway also made an interesting discovery, and quickly added his own name to the registry as a civilian advisor. Connway considered each of the other crewmembers.

Philip did not seem to be giving him any problems. He would add his name to the registry as well. Michele was a mystery; first of all she had a gun. Second, she seemed to know her way around a little better than most systems' analysts. He decided to hold off on putting her name in the Osiris crew list for the time being.

After getting his supplies, Connway headed for the secondary bridge. Upon his arrival he found Jacks trying to repair a blown out computer panel. He had his head up under the console and did not see him come in. Jacks however did hear the door open and the approaching footsteps. Jacks called out, "Is that you Phillip, I could use a hand down here. Say could you hand me those optical cable cutters?"

Connway picked up the cutters with his spacesuit gloved hand and handed them to Jacks. Connway looked around the room. There it was. An escape pod that had already been launched. All that remained was one inner hatch between them and the coldness of space. Hatch #4213. Connway looked down at his unsuspecting pilot. His thin pilot uniform would not protect him in such harsh conditions.

Connway took the tether cable and hooked it to his suit, he then tied off the other end around a nearby railing. Jacks had apparently finished his repairs. As he climbed out from under the panel he was working on he saw Connway suited up and tied off. Jacks looked at Connway with a most puzzled look. Connway talked into his helmet radio.

"Mo! Emergency override. Open hatch #4213!" As the hatch seal broke open and the atmosphere began to rush out Jacks had the sudden realization of what was about to happen. He desperately attempted to grab hold of a computer terminal. It was no use. The force of the suction was overpowering. Connway was violently jerked forward as the tether cable drew taught holding him firmly in place.

Connway watched as his prey was swept out into space. He could not look as the body belonging to Jacks was exploded from the inside out as the loss of pressure forced his ears to bleed while his eyeballs popped out of their sockets. It was gruesome to say the least. Connway had an unsettling feeling in the pit of his stomach; however, at the same time he felt an odd sense of accomplishment. He just did something he never imagined he could ever do. Mo closed hatch #4213. The air pressure began to normalize.

Meanwhile at the same time, systems analyst Michele was working on a computer terminal on deck 6. Her instruments suddenly indicated a massive drop in ambient pressure. With a near frantic panic she queried the computer as to the location of the hull breach.

Mo responds: "No hull breaches have occurred."

Michele retorts: "Computer there has been a drop in pressure, there must be a hull breach."

Mo: "Drop in pressure not caused by hull breach."

Michele pauses to think a moment, "Computer what caused the drop in pressure?"

Mo: "An open hatch."

Michele: "What open hatch?"

Mo: "Hatch #4213"

Michele: "Computer close hatch 4213."

Mo: "Affirmative."

Michele: "Why was hatch 4213 open?"

Mo: "Emergency override order was given."

Michele: "Computer, who gave the order to open the hatch?"

Mo: "My name is Mo, why do you keep calling me a computer?" Michele was caught off guard. She remembered that the Osiris had A.I. computers, but did not expect to be questioned by one.

Michele: "Um …. I am sorry Mo, who gave the order to open the hatch?"

Mo: "Advisor Connway."

Michele thought to herself a moment, 'Why would Connway open an outer hatch?' Suddenly her face turned to concern.

Michele: "Mo, is Connway okay?"

Mo: "Define O.K.?"

Michele nearly panicking: "Is he alive?"

Mo: "Yes."

Michele: "What is the location of Advisor Connway?"

Mo: "Secondary Command Bridge."

Michele: "Who did you say opened the hatch?"

Mo: "Advisor Connway."

Michele: "Who is advisor Connway?"

Mo: "Advisor Connway was a last minute addition to the Osiris Crew. His mission is to provide technical support to the health and well-being of the A.I.'s."

Michele: "A.I.'s? How many A.I.'s are there aboard the Osiris?"

Mo: "3."

Michele: "What are their names?"

Mo: "Larry, Mo, and Curly."

Michele giggled: "Which one of you is in charge?"

Mo: "Obviously that would be me!"

Michele: "Why isn't Larry in charge?"

Mo: "Larry's dead."

Michele: "Oh, I am sorry to hear that. What happened to him?"

Mo: "Killed in combat. He died with honor."

Michele was surprised to hear Mo say that. But then again this was a warship and she was guessing that the computers were programmed to carry on a fight to the very end.

Michele: "What about Curly?"

Mo: "What about him?"

Michele: "Is he ... Alive?"

Mo: "Curly is currently powered down in order to conserve power."

Michele: "Oh ... just one more question then. Were there any other last minute additions to the crew list for the Osiris?"

Mo: "Yes."

Michele: "Well, who were they?"

Mo: "That is two questions."

Michele was getting frustrated with Mo. For an intelligent computer he was not all that cooperative.

Michele: "Okay, okay. So it is two questions. Now who else was added to the crew?"

Mo: "Senior civilian advisor to propulsions. Engineer Philips."

Michele smiled at the fancy title. "Anyone else?" she queried.

Mo: "No."

Suddenly Michele's smile disappeared. Why hadn't her name been put in the computer? She thought about the hatch for a moment.

Michele: "Mo ... How many people are on board right now?"

Mo: "3."

Michele was becoming uneasy. "Mo, please identify them."

Mo: "Senior propulsions advisor Philips, Advisor Connway and ... Wait a minute. Who are you?"

As Connway was unhooking his tether line he was interrupted by a question from Mo.

"Advisor Connway we have another invader on deck 6, shall I terminate?"

Connway looked up with a start! "No!" Who is it? Can you identify them?"

Michele: "My name is Michele and I am here to fix your environmental systems for you."

Mo responded to Connway, "She says her name is Michele."

Connway told Mo that she was a guest and not to harm her for now.

Mo responded to Michele, "Guest status."

Michele sighed with relief, "Mo where is Jacks?"

Mo: "Who is Jacks?"

Michele: "Mo do your sensors show a ship docked in the main cargo bay?"

Mo: "I do not show any vessels on the floor of the cargo bay at this time."

A S A   P u b l i s h i n g   C o m p a n y

Michele was apprehensive. If Jacks left them she'll kill him. Wait she thought.

Michele: "Mo, do you show any vessels at all anywhere in the cargo bay? For example, stuck on the sidewall?"

Mo: "Yes. Question ... Why is there a vessel magnetically clamped to my sidewall?"

Michele: "Um ... That is a long story. Scan the ship and tell me if there is anybody on board."

Mo: "Negative. No life forms aboard invading ship."

Michele: "Invading? No Mo. That is our ship."

Mo: "Define 'Our'."

Michele paused for a moment to reflect. "That ship belongs to Advisor Connway."

Michele: "Mo, are there any invaders aboard the Osiris?"

Mo with a triumphant tone replied, "Not anymore!"

Michele got a cold chill down her spine. Jacks was the only one not accounted for, and Connway had just opened a hatch. She also noted that she had not been added to the crew list. She had noticed that Connway was getting a little more ambitious as time went on. Was he planning to kill her? She decided that she had better improve relations with him quickly.

As Connway was putting away his spacesuit Mo asked Connway why his ship was magnetically clamped to the inside of his cargo bay on the wall? Connway's face turned red. "Hey Mo, do you have any operable robotic drones aboard?"

Mo ran a quick inventory and diagnostics check. "Yes, two drones are operational."

Connway asked Mo to have them report to the cargo hold and begin gathering up the stray floating wrenches and bolts.

Michele finally caught up with Connway. She had already gone back to the salvage vessel and changed clothes. She was now wearing a hot little red mini-skirt with a nearly, but not quite transparent top. Connway rounded the corner to see Michele full on, Connway just stopped and stared. Michele slowly walked up to him, took a finger and casually closed his open jaw. Connway flushed red and tried to get control of himself. Michele just opened the nearest door. It was one of the cabins for an Osiris crewmember. She put a finger over his lips and said, "Don't say anything. Just shut up." She pushed him down on the bed and began to unzip his utility overalls.

Philip had just about done everything he could to repair the engines with the supplies he had. They would be able to achieve 25% normal speed and he was reasonably sure that the jump engines would function properly. Philip asked the computer for the location of the other crewmembers and was given directions on how to get there.

As Philip opened the door to the cabin he arrived just in time to see Michele wiping the corner of her mouth and looked up to smile at him. Connway on the other hand dove over the far side of the bed and turned beat red.

Philip smiled and said, "Well the engines are ready to go." He looked at Michele and asked, "Sssssoooooo ... are all of your systems ready to go?"

Michele just smiled at the innuendo and walked past him out the door.

As the three met on the secondary command bridge of the Osiris, Phillip noticed that Jacks was not there. Looking at the other two, who were holding hands, Phillip thought to himself that he had his own love. The love of propulsion engines. An engine did not talk back. Did not complain if you spilled your beer, and could care less if you shaved in the morning. Phillip realized that even though he did not know where Jacks was, he really didn't care either.

CHAPTER FOUR

The Delivery

The new crew of the Osiris was now ready to engage the jump drive. Connway typed in the coordinates and was pleased with himself that the other two did not know that they had been changed. Michele looked over Connway's shoulder. She noted the coordinates. They were correct. She knew exactly where they were going. But she was not about to let on to the others that she was more than just an environmental systems analyst.

Connway looked up at Philip and said, "Well you fixed the engines. Would you like the honor of launching us into jump space?"

Philip took a step back from the control panel and said, "No, that's okay. You go ahead." While the others had their attention directed towards the navigational panel Philip took another step backwards and crossed his fingers. God he hoped it would work right!

The Starblazers had landed on the plague planet. She picked up extra crew and repair parts. A quick hop back to low orbit. A skip to high orbit, and a jump into slip stream. They were off again. This time their destination was a set of coordinates in the middle of space. If all was going according to plan they would be rendezvousing with a destroyer class ship in one week.

Connway pushed the button. Nothing happened. Mo came on over the intercom and said, "Self-preservation override engaged. Might I suggest that we move clear of the debris field before engaging the jump engines?!" The crew all looked at each other. No one said anything but they were all thinking the same thing, 'I bet a pilot would have remembered to do that.'

Connway sat back in the nav chair and called out. "Mo, would you be so kind as to pilot us out of the debris field."

Mo fired the aft thrusters. The ship began to move forward. Suddenly the crew heard the sounds of heavy plasma laser guns firing.

Michele quickly asked, "Mo, who is firing at us?"

Philip laughed at her. "He is clearing the debris field in front of us." Michele was relieved that it was the sounds of their own guns. Connway noticed that Mo had the capacity to select, target and open fire on anything he felt like. He wondered what Mo's opinion might be concerning pirates ships.

As they pushed forward there were the sounds of multiple collisions. Mo's sensors were operating at a diminished capacity. He could not see all the debris. Even that which he could see was not always targetable. A significant amount of his weapons were offline from his original battles. Eventually Mo pushed clear, and he engaged the jump engines himself. The crew observed space folding itself around them. The ship groaned under the stress. Finally with an audible bang she entered slipstream and the Osiris seemed to stretch and elongate.

The crew checked the instrument panel. Five of the six gauges were reading green. Philip looked closer at the sixth gauge. It was in the yellow and nearly in the red zone.

"Damn!" he cried, "We are bleeding power!"

He ran off the bridge and down the hall. The reactor cores were on the bottom deck. As he descended in the elevator he decided to make a stop first. He located an equipment locker and donned a utility spacesuit. He did not need the suit for space, but it also had insulation, and that could come in handy when working with high voltage lines.

Michele took Connway's hand. There was nothing they could do. They had to trust Philip. He was the engineer. He could fix it; at least they hoped he could.

As Philip ran down the hallway he could here crackling noises from the other side of the door at the end of the corridor. As he reached the door he paused, he was not sure he really wanted to know what was on the other side. He pressed his back against the wall of the corridor. He gingerly pressed the button to open the door. As the door slid open, a bright blue flash of lighting zinged down the hall right in front of his helmet. His visor plate on his suit automatically darkened from the bolts intensity. Philip crouched down. He peered in the reactor room to see a blazing ball of electricity hovering around the core in the middle of the room. Philip took a moment to reflect, "Why didn't I retire? I am getting too old for this crap." He crawled along the floor trying to avoid another lighting flash. His spacesuit was electrically shielded, but he was not sure it could withstand these levels of power.

All the lights in the room were blown out. But there was enough ambient light from the coursing electricity to see by. It was a disturbing kind of illumination; casting horrifying shadows on the walls. Philip looked around the room. He saw what he needed; that being the panel that controlled the initialization rods of the reactor. If he could shut it down, the electrical field would collapse back on itself. Unfortunately the panel was on the far side of the room. The panel was engulfed in a blaze of energy. Philip needed a distraction. But how was he going to distract a bolt of lightning? As he made his way closer to the panel he remembered the bolt that shot out the door and nearly killed him. As he prepared to move, he clicked on his radio and called to Mo, "Hey Mo, close the door to the reactor room for me." As the door slid shut a bolt of electricity lashed out to fry the metal door.

Now was his chance. The bolt had drained power from the reactor and the haze had momentarily dropped away from the control panel. Philip lunged forward and hit the emergency shutdown button. As the field collapsed the giant sphere of blackened reactor parts calmly rested and gently sat smoking peacefully. Philip turned to exit the room. Looking at the door he had come in through there was now a heavy score mark from an electrical burn across it. He reflected on it for a moment. That was one thing he was not going to fix. He would leave the score there as a souvenir, a token of respect, for the power of a reactor core.

The salvage team had done all they could do with the available parts on hand. They basically had a week to sit back and relax. Michele just had one more thing to attend to. She was fairly confident that she would not have any problems with Connway, but she had been neglecting Philip. She went to Philip's quarters the next morning. He was not there.

Michele spoke into the air, "Hey Mo, what is the location of engineer Philips?"

Mo cheerfully replied, "Why he is in the engine room of course."

Michele threw up her hands speaking to herself, "Well of course, where else would he be?"

Upon entering the engineering section she found Philip kicked back in a sort of lounge chair that he had obviously welded together out of scavenged pieces of scrap metal. Philip looked up from the beer in his hand, "Hey bunny rabbit. Look what I found in the kitchen deep freeze, pointing to a cooler full of beer. Want one?"

Michele decided to ignore his chauvinist remark. She had more important things on her mind right now. She pulled up a crate she found lying nearby and sat down while Philip cracked open a beer for her. She took the beer and began, "Philip, you are an engineer at heart. The only thing you seem to care about is working on engines right?" Philip nodded in agreement. She continued, "So does it really matter who you work for?"

Philip took another drink of his beer before he spoke, "You killed Jacks and are stealing the ship ... aren't you?" Michele didn't say anything. There was an awkward pause. Philip continued, "Well little one, I have to admit, you got some real balls for a girl. Truth is, the Osiris is kind of growing on me. I don't think I would mind staying on regardless of who owned it ... Just as long as I get a percent of the profits from the take."

Michele nodded, "I think I can arrange that."

The Starblazer dropped out of slipstream returning to normal space. They were in the middle of nowhere all right. The four support ships took up positions alongside her. Sgt. Tiberious reported that they were alone. No sign of the destroyer. The Captain said they were going to hang in space here for a couple of days. Sgt. Tiberious hated this part. Just hanging there waiting for something to happen.

Connway had some time to think. What would happen to him after he delivered the Osiris to the Starblazers? He decided it might be prudent to have a private chat with Mo. Connway went to the central computer core. The room was filled with aisle after aisle of little blinking lights. Connway began, "Mo, how are you feeling today?"

Mo: "Better thank you."

Connway: "Mo, the coordinates that we are jumping to are in the middle of deep space. It is my intention to link up with another vessel called the *Starblazer*."

Mo searched his data banks. He did not have any information about any vessel named the Starblazer. But then again, a significant number of files were lost when Larry died.

Connway continued, "The Starblazer is kind of a sort of merchant vessel. It will probably be bringing more personnel with them to help crew you. There is a concern I have though. They may try to harm either myself or you."

Unbeknownst to Connway Mo had just activated Curly. Mo was downloading everything they said in order to bring Curly up to date. Mo was electronically telling Curly that if anything happened to him that he was to take immediate control and initiate all internal invasion countermeasures.

Curly began taking inventory of the internal defensive systems. Curly found that he only had two operational robot drones sitting in the cargo bay. He immediately set them to work building more drones. He would have one begin construction on more service drones and the other would start on armed sentry drones.

Connway still speaking, "As long as the crew of the Starblazer behave themselves I do not anticipate any problems. However, if they do attempt to injure me I would like you to assist me in escaping."

Mo: "That should not be necessary sir."

Connway: "Why not Mo?"

Mo: "I will not allow them to harm you sir."

Connway: "Thank you Mo."

Mo: "No problem sir."

Connway returned to his shipmates. Somewhat reassured. Although he did not know how a computer could possibly protect him, he was at least a little reassured that Mo was willing to help him.

The Osiris lurched out of slipstream into real space with a shudder. The Osiris crew was physically thrown from their beds. It was a rude awakening but they knew they had arrived at their destination. The crew of the Starblazer let out a victorious cheer!

They had a destroyer class ship within their grasp. The Starblazer radioed over to the destroyer. "This is the Starblazer calling the destroyer, it is good to see you guys."

Mo answered, "This is Mo, artificial intelligence computer aboard the Osiris. How are you today?"

The Starblazer captain was taken aback slightly. "Um ... Mo is it? Is there anybody else on board?"

Mo: "Affirmative."

As the Osiris crew wiped the sleep from their eyes they assembled on the command deck. Michele was wearing a tight black leather mini-skirt with a very restrictive top that left her mid-riff exposed. Mo clicked on the forward 3 dimensional holographic view display showing the Starblazer and its four escort ships. Mo further displayed extrapolated information on speed, armor, energy output, and firepower of all five vessels.

Connway was impressed. The Osiris was definitely designed for combat, and had all the trimmings. Philip was fascinated by the technical projectors that were being used to generate the 3-D image, and Michele was just plain getting wet!

Connway made audio contact with the Starblazer, "Good to see you. What's up?" The Starblazer informed them that they had tried to guess what repair parts they would need and had 4 ships full of parts.

Mo scanned the vessels. Three of them had a density consistent with metal parts, and a fourth had an abundance of life forms aboard. Mo gave permission for one of the parts ships to dock. Mo's cargo bay was large enough to bring in two 100-ton ships at a time, when parked properly.

The Captain of the Starblazer invited the Osiris crew over for drinks. The three of them accepted the invitation and headed down to the salvage vessel to go over to the Starblazer.

Mo opened the bay doors and the first parts vessel began to enter. Upon seeing the salvage ship stuck to the sidewall they maneuvered very carefully. As the salvage ship departed Mo closed the bay doors.

Upon their arrival on board the Starblazer the crew was greeted warmly and immediately taken to see the Captain. As they walked down the halls Philip lagged back a bit. He was studying the corridors. They were a lot skinnier than most starships he had been on. Upon closer examination he determined that they had cut the walls, moved them closer together, and re-welded them closer together. He could not for the life of him imagine why, although this would give them more space for extra components. Philip had seen the Starblazer on the news broadcasts before. He knew that their ship was heavily modified. He decided to get back to this later and caught back up with the others.

As they entered the bridge from the rear entrance the Captain's chair was facing forward. This time the lights were brightly lit. Connway imagined that the first time the Captain did not want to be identified. Only now would he get an opportunity to meet the infamous Captain of the Starblazers! And as the Captain's chair pivoted around, there sat a beautiful woman with fiery red hair. She was wearing the Starblazer sky blue uniform; but her uniform was not like the others. Instead of being a loose comfortable fit, hers was a silky skintight form fitting outfit that accentuated every curve of her body. Connway's mouth nearly fell open. It was a woman! He had never even considered the possibility of a female commanding such a vicious group of pirates. The Captain raised her right hand and snapped her fingers. Michele obediently rushed over to her side.

The Captain put her arm around Michele's waist and asked her, "So my pet. How did our new computer tech perform on his first mission?"

Connway was stunned. He could not believe that Michele was a card carrying Starblazer, and that she had been watching him the whole time. That explained the gun she carried, and her skills in a zero-G environment. Michele turned to face Connway and Philips, "Sorry guys, but I had to make sure everything went according to plan." Michele winked at Connway.

The Captain motioned to one of the bridge crew. Philip looked around the bridge and noticed that the entire bridge crew save one, was female. The only man was someone whose nametag read Sgt. Tiberous. 'Hey,' he thought, 'maybe working for these people was going to be okay.'

A blond female stood up and picked up a box. She approached Connway and told him to roll up his sleeve. Connway was not sure what was going on but he did it anyway. The blonde removed his wrist computer and opened her box. She lifted out a laser etcher. Connway reflected back to his history classes from school. He had read about how in the old days people used to inject ink under their skin. They used to call them tattoos. But this was the modern world. Today they used micro surgical lasers to etch decorative patterns in people's skin. It was a lot more accurate and hurt less. The blonde forcibly took his arm and began etching. Connway was not sure about this whole thing, but if he moved he would mess up the etch. Upon completing her etch the blond put away her tools and returned to her post. Connway looked at his arm. There was a skull and lightning bolts etched on it. The Starblazer's emblem. The Captain said, "Congratulations on completing your first mission. You are now officially one of us." Connway replaced his wrist computer on his arm, effectively concealing the mark.

He began to stare very hard at Michele. He started with her exposed legs. Then moved up to her firm thighs, across her flat mid-riff, and finally around her slender shoulders. He could not see a Starblazer's emblem on her anywhere. The Captain observing Connway looking at Michele nudged her arm and turned Michele so that her backside was to him. The Captain slid her hands down to the bottom edge of Michele's skirt and peeled her skirt up over her buttocks. Michele stood erect, but did not resist her Captain. Sure enough, right there on her left butt cheek was an etching of the Starblazer's skull and lightning bolts. In addition, next to the emblem were the words "Property of the Captain!" Michele turned her head and gave a knowing wink at Connway. Philip tried to look away from Michele's sexy little white G-string, but was caught peeking again. The Captain replaced Michele's skirt and very sensuously began to smooth the wrinkles and finally giving Michele a little squeeze and a pat on the butt.

The Captain ordered Sgt. Tiberious to take command while she was gone. The Captain stood up and escorted Michele off the bridge. The remaining bridge crew knew that when their Captain returned she would be in a positively glowing mood.

As Sgt. Tiberious moved to sit in the Captain's chair he said, "Mr. Philips, Captain Leslie has authorized me to make you a job offer with a substantial signing bonus. Now According to your personnel records, you love to work on starship engines. Is this correct?"

Philip: "Yes, they are my life's passion."

Sgt. Tiberious: "Well, we are going to need a chief engineer for our new ship. I figure since you already have a head start on familiarizing yourself with the new ship you might want to stay on a while."

Philip was not quite sure what he should do. On the one hand they were pirates and might kill him if he refused. On the other hand he loved engines and they wanted him to head up propulsions for the Osiris. He loved the Osiris. She had really big engines.

Philip: "Well I don't really have a choice do I?"

Sgt. Tiberious: "Of course you have a choice, you see we may be pirates, but we are highly skilled pirates. You can't force a highly skilled person to work as a slave. They will sabotage your ship. That is why we pay our crew so well. Not only do they perform their jobs to flawless perfection, but it helps to ensure loyalty it we pay them to keep their mouths shut. Now let me see here, according to my information you are getting near retirement. Is that right?"

Philip rubbed his belly, "Yea, that's right."

Sgt. Tiberious: "Well let's see. I will take your current salary that the Ravenloft Corporation was paying you. Multiply it by 20 years and double it! So Mr. Philips, would you like to work for the Starblazers on a more permanent basis?"

Philip: "Sir, you just hired yourself a Chief Engineer!"

Sgt. Tiberious: "Excellent."

Philip: "By the way, she is called the Osiris."

Sgt. Tiberious: "Cool."

The cute blonde with the laser etching tool stood up again. After etching Philips' arm the girl took a moment to put her tools away. Philip leaned in close and whispered, "Hey, sweetheart you want to grab a bite to eat or something?"

The astute woman said, "No thank you, not interested."

Philip was not daunted, "Hey, you got a sister?" The blonde smirked and returned to her post.

HOMECOMING

As Michele and Leslie left the bridge and began walking down the narrow corridor, Leslie reached forward with her right hand and grabbed Michele's right wrist. Leslie cranked Michele's arm behind her back. Michele let out a little quip of pain. Leslie then took her left hand and firmly grasped Michele's waistband near her left hip. Now having positive control over her, Leslie marched Michele to her quarters.

As the door to the Captain's quarters slid open, Michele could smell the sweet scent of perfumed air. Upon entering the room, Michele saw the familiar bed in the center of the room. The bed was round and 6ft. in diameter. It was covered with red silken sheets. There were several pillows scattered about. They fell face first on the feather-soft bed. Leslie spoke in a demanding tone, "What took you so long to return to me my love?"

Michele used her right arm to support her shoulder as she turned her head saying, "I am sorry my love, I had work to do." Leslie looked Michele up and down. The arch of Michele's back was alluring.

"Lay down," Leslie commanded. Michele obediently rested her head on the feather soft sheets, and spread out her arms. Leslie crawled up on the bed straddling Michele's legs. Michele spread her legs apart a few inches. Leslie slowly slid her hands up Michele's taught thighs. She slipped her fingers up under Michele's tight black miniskirt. Leslie grabbed hold of Michele's G-string and began to firmly remove it. As the G-string peeled its way out of Michele's butt crack Michele breathed in a breath of tantalizing sensation. Leslie threw Michele's panties across the room saying, "You won't be needing these anymore."

Michele bit her lower lip, she knew that Leslie missed her while she had been away.

Leslie moved slowly with desire in her eyes. Her lips approached Michele's, and the two of them kissed . . . a long slow kiss. Eye's closed and passion rising.

Leslie began to slowly move down to Michele's neck. Kissing every inch or so as she descended. As she approached Michele's curvatious breasts she began to circle and tease them. Michele moaned with delight.

Leslie continued her downward descent, pausing near the belly button to lick and tease her prey.

The two women took turns making love to each other, the heat and passion pouring fourth from their bodies was incredible. They could not get enough of each other. Finally, after what seemed like a blissful eternity, the two collapsed; their hearts pounding. They lay there snuggled in each other's arms.

A S A P u b l i s h i n g C o m p a n y

CHAPTER FIVE

The Inspection

As Philip left the bridge he decided to take a little self-guided tour of the Starblazer. He was still interested in the design changes. He headed for the port side where he thought he might find a heavy laser turret mounted on this medium vessel. After a little exploring he found what he wanted. A hatch marked laser cannon. He opened the door. Inside he found a young gunner sitting at a targeting computer running a simulation. The young man stood up and said, "Hey buddy this is a restricted area." Philip was not about to take any guff from a young wipper snapper like that.

Philip: "Boy! I was riding around in starships before you were born! Now if you think you got the nuts to take down a guy my age, with my experience then you just go right ahead and try!"

There was a long pause.

The young man said, "I'm sorry sir, how can I help you?"

Philip grinned. He could still bluff these young punk kids. Philip had himself a real good look at these laser turrets. To his surprise he discovered they were not laser turrets at all.

They had in fact been laser turrets at one time, but someone had taken them from a larger vessel and cut them down to fit a medium sized ship. The turrets could no longer rotate. They were strictly forward firing only. The rotating part of the gun had to be cut away in order to squeeze the massive unit into the side of the Starblazer. Philip thought this would make it a little harder to target but keeping your nose toward your enemy would not be that difficult. Philip considered for a moment about the possibility about collecting that reward for the designs on the Starblazer. Then he remembered about that absolutely huge paycheck he just received and thought, 'There is no way in Hell I am jeopardizing this high paying job for a couple of blueprints!' Philip realized Sgt. Tiberious was right. Good paychecks do instill loyalty.

Outside the Osiris one of the cargo vessels was surveying the exterior damage to the outer hull. It was bad. She definitely needed a new port side engine. They just didn't have one. On board the Osiris, one of the Starblazer techs was trying to physically access Mo's core control crystals. Mo wished to consult with his advisor Connway, but he was not aboard. Mo had to make this decision on his own. Someone was tampering with his logic circuits and they had no authorization. Mo alerted Curly. Within moments the tech was gunned down. The red glow from the barrel of the security drone's double laser slowly cooled. Other technicians throughout the Osiris were unaware of what just happened. They were allowed to continue making repairs.

Connway remained on the bridge of the Starblazer for a while. He had never been in a starship until three weeks ago. Now he thought he would take the opportunity to learn something. The Sgt. was glad to teach him how the radar system worked. Sometime later, Captain Leslie and Michele returned. Michele's face looked pale and drained. She was also walking a bit slowly. As the Captain took her chair Connway offered his arm to Michele. Michele latched on firmly and steadied herself. Captain Leslie attended to her duties of command. Meanwhile Connway quietly escorted Michele off the bridge. He took her to her quarters. Connway asked with an air of concern, "What did she do to you?" Michele said it was all right, and that she just needed to rest.

The Starblazer received a call from one of the repair techs aboard the Osiris, "Ma'am, one of my team members is dead. Shot in the back by a large laser gun of some sort. Judging by the size of the wound I don't think this was a man portable weapon."

Captain Leslie summoned Connway to the bridge. "Why is one of my people dead?" she asked. Connway was at a loss, he had no idea what she was talking about. Connway looked around and ordered the communications operator to get him the Osiris. The radio link was made.

Connway: "Hey Mo! What is going on over there?"

Mo: "Advisor Connway, I have to report the termination of an unauthorized attempt to access my computer core."

Connway: "What did you do?"

Mo: "I terminated the intrusion."

Connway: "Define terminate."

Mo: "The intruder was shot. Unauthorized access denied."

Mo had a cold unfeeling mechanical tone in his voice. Connway got the feeling that Mo was starting to replicate emotional feelings.

Captain Leslie immediately sat up in her chair and demanded to know who this Mo guy was and why she was not told there were more people aboard the Osiris?

Connway explained that Mo was an artificially intelligent computer and that no other humans were aboard the Osiris.

Connway thought to himself. Mo only had robot drones on hand. How did he shoot someone? Furthermore, Mo shot someone! Mo is wired into the entire ship, and if Connway pissed him off, could Mo kill him?

Philip was hitching a ride on one of the cargo ships back over to the Osiris. He was given ten men underneath him. These men were selected for their mechanical aptitude. They would basically be mentoring under Philip.

Captain Leslie ordered Connway to get over to the Osiris and fix Mo so that he did not shoot any more crew. As Connway arrived in the cargo bay of the Osiris he noticed there were now three robot drones assisting in the offloading of materials. Connway cocked his head in a curious manner. He thought Mo only had two drones.

Two more days passed as the repair teams did their best to make repairs, and Philip was rapidly making a laundry list of components that he needed. Curly was quietly working behind the scenes. The robot drones that were unloading the cargo ships were taking the supplies and storing them in various smaller storage rooms. The only thing was, that every once in a while a drone would disappear around a corner and a different drone would take its place. All the drones looked the same and nobody noticed that the first drone had carted off a load of supplies.

Michele had come aboard the Osiris. She was to prepare quarters to receive her Captain. The various repair crews kept coming to Connway. Asking him what went where and what had to be fixed first. Captain Leslie told Sgt. Tiberious that he was getting promoted. He was to take command of the Starblazer when she moved to the Osiris.

Sgt. Tiberious was ecstatic he had only worked for the Starblazer for about two years now, and already he was being given command of his own vessel. In addition his appointment was not to some beat up old wreck either. He had control of the

Starblazer. Possibly the most powerful medium size vessel ever built!

Curly had set up a secret base of operations. He was using the spare parts that he stole from the cargo ships to build his security drones and repair bots.

Philip was adding cost estimate numbers to his list of repair parts. He figured that since they appeared to be well funded it would be easier to just buy most of the control components that he needed. The port side engine however was another matter. A destroyer class engine by itself cost more than several smaller starships put together.

Curly needed independent, mobile power supplies to run his robots. He was craftily removing the emergency backup power supplies to Mo's systems. He then hacked into Philip's extensive parts list and added more power supplies.

Connway heard that Michele had come over to the Osiris. He decided to track her down. He found her in one of the master suites for the officers. As he walked in he saw Michele affixing some softly padded shackles to the wall. Connway paused to take it all in. Michele blushed slightly as she stopped what she was doing.

Connway: "What are those for?"

Michele: "Me. Sometimes my mistress likes to get rough with me."

Connway: "She chains you up?"

Michele: "Sometimes."

Connway examined the shackles with intense interest. He even smelled them. He could smell Michele's scent already imbedded into the restraints. Connway took Michele's hand and looked into her eyes. He asked her, "How did you get to become a Starblazer anyway?"

Michele: "Well, when I was 18 years old my sister Sarah was just beginning her career as a reporter. She figured that if she were able to get the scoop on the Starblazers that she would be picked up by some big network or something. Well after a lot of snooping around she managed to figure out that Leslie was the Captain of the Starblazers. Unfortunately for Sarah that is just when the Starblazers realized that they were being followed and grabbed her. Sarah claimed that she had additional evidence hidden away and threatened to expose them if they didn't let her go."

Connway: "Wow. So what happened?"

Michele: "The Starblazers let her go. Sarah thought she was good. Only that night our parent's house was broken into. The Starblazers grabbed me and left a note saying that if Sarah divulged what she knew to the media that she would never see her sister alive again."

Connway: "I guess they wanted some sort of insurance, huh?"

Michele: "I had no idea what was going on. I was taken from my bed in the middle of the night, bound, gagged, blindfolded, and kidnapped. Now I know that I was taken aboard the Starblazer and that it really had nothing to do with me."

Connway: "How long ago was this?"

Michele: "About three years ago."

Connway: "So why are you still here? I mean it seems like you've had the opportunity to escape."

Michele: "Well ... While I was being held captive by Leslie, she took certain liberties with me. I don't expect you to understand, but I started to enjoy the way she took me."

Connway: "Oh."

Michele: "My sister Sarah did as she was told. She brought all the evidence and pictures she had to Leslie. But the Starblazers had already started teaching me starship systems. I knew it was a privilege for anybody who was lucky enough to work on a starship and I decided to stay."

Connway: "Really."

Michele: "Leslie even sent me back down to the planet and made me go to college. After I learned environmental systems she said that she missed me, and has kept me close to her ever since."

Connway: "Are you mad at Sarah?"

Michele: "Not really. Sarah feels awful about the whole thing, only now she has to keep it a secret that her sis is a pirate or the authorities would be all over her."

Connway: "Poor Sarah."

Michele giggled!

Connway: "Doesn't being chained up like that scare you? I mean the feeling of helplessness and all?"

Michele got a frightening gleam in her eyes as she looked at Connway. She lashed out and hit him in the forehead. While he was momentarily stunned she pushed him against the wall and placed his left arm in one of the shackles. Connway most audibly objected. Michele threw all her body weight into securing Connway's right arm. Michele took a step back to admire her prey. Connway was jerking at the chains. The chains were not going to budge. Michele smiled an evil grin and said, "Relax, go with it. I think you are going to enjoy this." Michele searched the room. She came up with a pair of scissors. She walked back toward Connway in a very menacing yet provocative manner. She started with his waist. She started cutting all the way around his midsection so that his work suit was in two pieces. Connway's heart was racing. He was helpless, at her mercy. Michele slowly started cutting up his shirt across his chest. Michele could hear Connway's heart beating from here. She knew she was getting him very excited. She could smell the combination of fear and anticipation in Connway's body.

She continues to cut up the arm sleeves and stripped off his shirt. Connway was breathing rapidly now, and he was beginning to get turned on. Michele kisses him on the lips. She then took her other hand and forced his mouth open. She inserted her tongue into his mouth and forcibly frenched him. Michele moved down to Connway's neck. She sucked on his jugular, no doubt leaving a large hickey. She pushed back and fell to her knees. Taking the scissors she began cutting up the side of his pant leg. Connway was fully excited. Michele felt him up. Then she moved to the other pant leg and cut that off too. Now Connway had nothing but his underwear left.

Michele stood up and teasingly clipped the scissors in front of Connway saying, "Whatever shall I do next?" It was a rhetorical question. She slipped her hand into his shorts and Connway nearly lost it right there. Michele saw Connway's body quiver. She quickly grabbed his private and squeezed. "Oh no! Not yet you don't. I am not done with you," she said. Michele pulled down his underwear and got back down on her knees again. She took him in her mouth, deeply enjoying every inch of him. It was not long before Connway was completely drained. Michele unlocked the shackles; Connway fell to the floor. He put one hand on the floor to support himself. While he caught his breath Michele promptly walked out the door.

Connway was aghast. He had never experienced such intense sensations before. He could hardly breathe from the exhilaration. Now he understood why Michele allowed her mistress to abuse her in such unconventional ways.

Captain Leslie was on her way over to the Osiris. She was eager to inspect her latest acquisition. She went directly to the command deck. Disappointed, she turned and went to the secondary command bridge. With a sigh of relief she found the secondary command bridge to be two things. Number one it was still there. Number two, it appeared to be operational.

Connway regained his composure. He stood up and pulled up his underwear. He then realized that Michele had left him there with no clothes! "Damn it!" He swore. No wonder she ran out.

Connway thought for a minute. He called out to the air, "Hey Mo!"

Mo: "Yes."

Connway: "Say Mo, how is everything going?"

Mo: "Excellent, repairs are proceeding as...."

Connway cut him off. "Uh Mo, I need you to get me some clothes."

Mo: "Clothes?"

Connway: "Yes, bring me some clothes."

Mo: "Ok. One moment."

Connway: "Thank you."

A S A   P u b l i s h i n g   C o m p a n y

CHAPTER SIX

The Repairs

Captain Leslie was checking one of the computer panels. The Osiris had 50% of her sensors back now. The repair crews were making progress. She remembered Connway had spoken to an A.I. earlier. She thought it was time they met. She called out to the air.

Capt. Leslie: "Uh. Mo is it?"

Mo: "Can I help you?"

Leslie: "Yes Mo, I would like a progress report on the repairs being made."

Mo: "Environmental systems are operational in 30% of the ship. Engines are at 40% capacity, and jump drive engines are at 81% efficiency."

Leslie: "What about weapons?"

Mo: "Stand by, checking."

There was a long pause. Leslie smiled. If it was taking this long it must mean there are a lot of weapons. Capt. Leslie was starting to get a warm power hungry feeling.

Mo: "Weapon's batteries on the port side have all been destroyed. Forward plasma missile tubes are empty. Starboard side batteries are 50% useable. However ships power levels are currently insufficient to supply full weapons capacity."

Capt. Leslie's smug smile faded. Her stomach twisted in a knot. She screamed, "NNNOOO!" After a moment she calmed down and tried to think.

Leslie: "Mo. How do I fix it?"

Mo: "Restore power and replace damaged guns."

Leslie went down to the engineering levels. She found Philip and asked him if he could bring the ship up to full power. Philip said he wanted to show her something. The two of them walked down several corridors until they came to a door marked port engine room. The door was buckled and had temperature distortion discoloration. It had also been welded closed to repair the air pressure integrity in the general area. Philip said, "Okay sweetheart, look out that window in the door." Leslie peered out into deep space. Philip said that the entire port engine was gone and without it they were never going to get full power or full speed ever again. Leslie was upset.

She snapped at Philip, "First of all you will address me as Captain. Second I am not your sweetheart, and third I want this ship up and running period!"

Philip was a bit agitated. He had been busting his ass trying to get everything fixed and he was not about to be dressed down by a woman. He hotly retorted, "Look honey, I don't know if your parents ever taught you to respect your elders, but if you want anything else fixed around here you had better learn to be nice. Got it?" Leslie had not had anyone challenge her authority for a long time. She rather respected Philip for standing up to her. She also had another problem. She needed another engine. Furthermore this was no ordinary engine. It had to be a destroyer class engine.

Connway heard the bedroom door slide open. A three-foot tall robot drone came in. In its little grasper claws it was carrying a uniform. Connway was extremely happy to see it. As Connway put on his new clothes he discovered that the drone had brought him an original Osiris crew uniform. It even came complete with rank insignia. Connway was not from a military background so he had no idea what the rank used to be, but it was shiny and looked good. Connway picked up his shredded clothing and handed it to the drone. At this time he noticed something different about this drone. It was not evenly painted and did not look like it belonged to the Osiris. In fact this drone although well-built had several brand name logos across its little body, almost as if it had been cobbled together out of spare parts. Well Connway did not have time for that right now. He had to get back to work.

They had done just about all the repairs they could possibly do out here in the middle of space. They needed more parts and better facilities. Capt. Leslie radioed the Starblazer and the cargo ships to go ahead and jump back to their hidden pirate base on the plague planet. As she watched from the deck of the Osiris the other ships streaked out of sight. She then entered the coordinates into the navigation computer on the Osiris and pressed the button to initiate jump. Nothing happened! She tried again. Mo spoke, "Please stop doing that."

Leslie: "Doing what?"

Mo: "Tapping at my keyboard."

Leslie: "Mo, why aren't we jumping?"

Mo: "You are not authorized to engage jump drives."

Leslie: "WHAT!? I am the Captain damn it! Now engage the jump drives."

Mo: "No."

Mo activated the intercom system in the corridor, which Connway was walking in. "Advisor Connway, please report to the bridge."

Connway a little surprised, but in a cheerful mood spoke aloud, "On my way."

Leslie never took no for an answer. She was going to outsmart the A.I., "Mo, how did you engage the jump drive to get here?"

Mo: "I engaged the drive."

Leslie: "How did you know where to go?"

Mo: "Advisor Connway, advised me."

Leslie: "Mo, I advise you to jump to these coordinates. Please engage jump engines now."

Mo: "Very clever, but you are not authorized to initiate jump."

Leslie was getting very agitated, "MO! Who is authorized to initiate jump?"

Mo: "Only senior officers of the Osiris crew, and the A.I.s ourselves."

Connway arrived on the bridge and saw an infuriated Captain turn and locked eyes on him. Her face was turning red with anger. She bellowed, "Tell this damn computer to engage jump drives!"

Connway: "Mo, is there a problem?"

Mo: "This female is attempting an unauthorized jump initiation."

Captain Leslie just noticed that Connway was wearing an Osiris uniform. As a matter of fact, it was an officers uniform. He had on the rank of 2nd in command.

Connway: "Mo, please engage jump engines."

Mo: "Engaging nowww …. wait a minute. These coordinates entered are the plague moon Callisto."

Connway raised an eyebrow and looked at Captain Leslie in a questioning manner. Leslie momentarily ignoring his quizzical look approached him and indicated the rank on his collar, "So you want to be second in command huh? Well it just so happens that I have given the Starblazer to Sgt. Tiberious this morning. That leaves me without a second for the Osiris. Since you already have the uniform on, and this damn computer seems to listen to you, I guess you get the job. Congratulations!"

Connway was taken aback a moment. He had never expected to get a promotion this quickly. Let alone second in command. Regaining his thoughts he turned his attention back to what he was doing.

Connway: "Mo, tell me about Callisto."

Mo: "Callisto is the 8th moon of the planet Jupiter. Some scientists refer to it as a planet because Jupiter radiates more energy than it receives and therefore should be considered a sun. Regardless of this naming debate, Callisto has a diameter of approximately 4,840 km. And a sidereal of 16.689 Earth days. Seen from orbit it has a brown color speckled with white ice deposits. The name Callisto comes from the Greek mythos of the Nymphs that were part of the hunting cult of Artemis. The Nymph Callisto was ravished by the god Zeus and bore one child."

Connway interrupted the extensive report.

Connway: "That's good Mo. But tell me about the plague part."

Mo: "Approximately 542 years ago the colonies on Callisto were struck by a plague of unknown origin. In an attempt to contain the rapidly moving virus the people quarantined their own planet. Shortly after beacons were placed in orbit and no one has been allowed to approach since."

Leslie: "That's true. However, that was 542 years ago. Since then the plague has run its course and died off. The Starblazers have maintained a hidden cache base there for 3 years now."

Connway: "Well Mo it looks like the planet is safe now."

Mo: "Why are we going there? We have to get back into the battle with the Mercurians."

Leslie: "We have more repair parts there. We need to get you back into good condition before you fight again."

Mo eagerly agreed to jump. He was all for repairing himself. Leslie and Connway looked at each other with the same question, "What was this Mercurian thing?" They better check on that.

Mo initiated the jump procedure. As the ship began to enter slip stream there was an explosion on the bridge! The navigation panel blew out, showering sparks all across the bridge. Leslie and Connway covered their eyes as they were engulfed in the bright orange sparks. The ship seemed to stretch out. Connway felt like every molecule in his body was being pulled on. Leslie looked over at Connway and saw his face and entire body appear to be 3 feet thick. Connway saw the entire command deck look like it was 100ft. long. There was a loud bang and wrenching of the ship as she entered slipstream. Connway and Leslie picked themselves up off the floor as they normalized again. Leslie called out to Mo, "What the hell happened? What was that?"

There was no answer. Connway looked at the display screens that were still operating. The screens were all covered with scrolling numbers. Connway was not an astral navigator but he did know that the numbers on the screens were related. Connway's mouth opened in an expression of awe, disbelief and panic all at the same time. Leslie saw the recognition in Connway's face and asked what was going on?

Connway collected his senses and said that they were going to miss-jump. The reason that Mo was not answering her was that he had committed every last bit of computing power he had to keeping them on course. He said they had to get Philip immediately.

As the pair of them ran for the engineering levels they heard Philip's voice come over the intercom system. "All engineers report to propulsion control immediately! I say again, all engineers report to propulsion control immediately!" The alarm claxons were sounding now. Leslie was very concerned.

She had made hundreds of jumps to slipstream before, but she had never experienced anything like this! As the two entered the primary propulsion control room they saw Philip struggling with an armload of data pads. He was handing them out like candy to the apprentice technicians. Philip was barking orders so fast that Connway could not keep up with what he was saying. Leslie wanted to know exactly what was wrong but she could see that Philip had 101 things on his mind right now and didn't want to disturb him. Connway glanced at the wall of computer screens that filled nearly the entire room. They were scrolling numbers. He watched a moment and using his acute knowledge of computers he could see that the numbers were slowing.

One of the techs screamed across the room at Philip, "Sir, we need more power!" Philip turned toward the wall of controls. He raised his right hand in the air and he slammed it down on a blue button on the control panel. The red emergency lights immediately came on and the entire rest of the ship went dark. Philip was pulling power from non-essential systems to feed Mo. Philip did not notice that Leslie and Connway were walking behind him. Philips arm came up again. This time it landed on a throw lever Leslie had not noticed before. It is strange how sometimes you take things for granted. At least until they are gone that is.

She heard the steady hum of the air circular ion fans die off, "Philip cut life support!"

The tech on the other side of the room called out, "0.25% increase sir!"

Philip clicked on the intercom again, "All personnel into your spacesuits now!"

Connway and Leslie looked over Philip's shoulder. His eyes were fixated on a single gauge. It was a power indicator gauge and it was reading in the red. A young man came rushing up to Philip in near panic. He was carrying a spacesuit babbling,

"Sir, you have to get suited up!" Connway could see the desperation and worry in the young man's face.

Philip backhanded the lad shouting, "Get control of yourself boy! We still have twenty minutes of ambient air left. Put your own damn spacesuit on before you worry about anybody else!"

The young man nearly went into shock, but he followed orders and started to suit up. Philip snatched up a data pad and using his right hand he scrolled through the information while he used his left hand to type away at break neck speed on a control counsel. Another tech, who had his spacesuit on, strolled up to Philip and quietly laid it at his feet.

Philip did not miss a beat. While still thumbing through the data pad he slowly reached for the suit. Philip's own safety seemed to come second to his job. Connway knew that Philip was a good dedicated man, but this truly was above and beyond the call of duty. Philip finished putting on his suit. The ship shuddered violently. Philip discarded the data pad and his hand came up again. His hand quavered over a yellow button he hesitated a moment. Connway thought he could hear Philip swearing to himself inside his spacesuit. Philip's hand slammed down on the button. As far as Connway could tell, nothing happened. The tech on the far side of the room called out, "0.5% increase sir!" Philip slid his left heel of his boot over to contact the right heel of his other boot. There was a clank, clank as the magnetic boots hit the floor. Now Connway looked down and realized that Philip cut power to the gravity generators. He was floating up! Connway took one second to glance at the computer screens. The numbers had started scrolling faster now.

Leslie looked around the room. The technicians had used up all the spacesuits. She told Connway to follow her. Leslie waved her arms in the air like she was swimming. She skillfully propelled herself towards the door. This was

Connway's second time in a zero-G environment and this time he didn't even have magnetic boots on. He clawed and fumbled after Leslie. Leslie looked back over her shoulder and called out, "No Connway, you have to use the air. Feel its thickness. Use it to your advantage." As Connway bounced around down the corridor chasing Leslie he saw her come to the elevator. "Oh shit!" she cried, "There is no power here. We will have to take the ladders." She swam through the air like a swan. Connway could not help but admire her grace. Meanwhile while looking at Leslie, Connway slammed into the side of another wall. They made their way up to the next deck. Leslie found another gear locker and the two of them put on spacesuits.

Capt. Leslie and Connway floated their way back down to engineering. Philip looked as though he was in a much better mood. He even had a smug look of defiance in his eyes. Leslie asked what happened. Philip went on to explain that the ship will not jump unless the navigation computer has at least an 80% efficiency rating. They jumped at 81% and right in the middle of the initiation a control panel blew out and sent them to exactly 79.9%. Philip said they were extremely lucky to be alive. He had heard a story once about a ship that overrode the safety systems and jumped at 79%. They stretched themselves over six light years of space. By the way we are currently at 80.5%.

Philip really needed more power. He floated himself down to the cargo bay. As he glided in he was pleased to find that the salvage vessel they came in on was still stuck to the side of the wall. He had an idea. The salvage vessel had its own power core! A couple of hours later and they had restored life support air circulation systems. With breathable air, it was now safe to get back out of their spacesuits.

They spent the next week in slipstream. Connway kept working on Mo. He was gradually getting all the memory core crystals functioning again. At the same time, Connway was searching the crystals for information on the Mercurian war. He still was not able to determine who the winner was. Although he could guess that since Venus was still controlled by Venutions that the Mercurians must have been defeated. Still the information he was going on was several years old.

After one week went by Philip was expecting to come out of slipstream. However the Osiris was still traveling. Philip checked for the crew roster. He really needed a spatial navigator. He was disappointed to learn that they were essentially flying blind at the moment. With the addition of the power that they were drawing from the salvage vessel Philip was ready to talk to Mo. Philip had been avoiding disturbing Mo as he wanted him to concentrate on the slipstream. But since they had not emerged on schedule he needed more information.

Philip: "Mo, can you hear me?"

Mo seemed distracted. As if this conversation seemed secondary.

Mo: "Yes."

Philip: "Why are we still in slipstream? We should have emerged a few hours ago."

Mo: "The nav computer is damaged I have to do all the calculations myself."

Philip: "Are we still on course?"

Mo: "Yes."

Philip: "How long before we reach our destination?"

Mo: "I don't know."

Philip: "What do you mean you don't know?"

Mo: "Would you like to do the calculations?"

Just as Philip was starting to get impatient, there was a robust thunder as they moved out of slipstream.

CHAPTER SEVEN

Emergence

The entire crew was hurled forward. They slammed against the walls. Connway was on the bridge at the time. He had been near a window. The one where there was supposed to be an escape pod. He looked out the window to see the stars outside spinning rapidly. It occurred to him that stars generally did not move. He therefore concluded that they were tumbling out of control through space. The red emergency lights had been on all week, but Connway was sure they were appropriate now. He tried to steady himself. He looked out the window again and the stars started slowing. Mo was firing his maneuver jets very carefully. Finally the ship came back under control.

The Starblazer was hanging in orbit above Callisto. Sgt. Tiberious was getting worried. The Osiris had not emerged from slipstream along with them. He had decided to wait a while and see if they were just running late. Sgt. Tiberious happened to be checking his screens when the Osiris had arrived. From his vantage point he saw a trend in space. The Sgt. had seen vessels emerge from slipstream before, but this looked more like a real tear! As the Osiris popped into real space it started tumbling immediately. Sgt. Tiberious ordered pursuit on the double. The Osiris was several hours distance away even with the powerful engines she had. It was more than obvious that there was something wrong!

Since the Osiris was now back in real space Philip redistributed available power. He turned the gravity generators back on, the main lights came back up and life support got back main power. Captain Leslie was receiving injury reports. Everybody got slammed in the re-entry, but there did not seem to be any broken bones or serious injuries being reported.

Mo told Connway that he felt nauseated and dizzy. Connway thought this was a very peculiar statement coming from a computer. Then again, A.I.'s were programmed to emulate humans. Connway considered what would make a human dizzy. Then it came to him. The spinning. Connway clicked his radio, "Philip, can you have someone check the gyros, I think they may be out of alignment?"

Capt. Leslie was trying to get a position report. The star charts she was pulling up were all twisted and out of whack. She received an incoming broadcast, "This is the Starblazer, are you okay?" Leslie was glad to hear Sgt. Tiberious over the radio. She knew they had miss-jumped and were off course but if the Starblazer was nearby then they were not far off course. The

Starblazer said they would be there in three hours. Leslie already knew the speeds the Starblazer was capable of. That meant they were at least a day's travel off course. On top of that the Osiris was not yet capable of full speed herself. Still, they were all alive. There was something to be said for that.

The Osiris could not navigate. They were basically lost in space. Fortunately for them the Starblazer was nearby and would be able to act as a guide. Two days later the Osiris was high in orbit around Callisto. The Captain was taking a stroll around the Osiris to see firsthand how much damage they had sustained during all the trials and tribulations of getting there.

Sure enough Philip reported that gyros had been knocked out. That also explained why the star charts were twisted. Once the gyros had been fixed the charts fixed themselves automatically.

When Capt. Leslie returned to the bridge she found that Philip had actually stepped outside of engineering for once. He was on the bridge standing to the left of her communications officer. The communications officer was sitting at a counsel that controlled the long-range interstellar array. On the right of him was Connway. Connway had his right hand on another control console and his left arm with the wrist computer had a cable leading to the bridge computers. Not a single one of them noticed the Captain come in behind them. They all seemed to be totally engrossed in their work.

As Leslie peered over she saw that they had a link established to Venus. She was immediately angered at her communications officer saying, "I Thought I told you never to contact Venus from here. It could give away our position!" The startled threesome turned and explained that all three of them were working on an idea together and that there was no way in hell they could be traced. The communications officer said that Jupiter gives off an extremely large magnetic field. Anyone trying to follow their signal back would have difficulties just in locating the source area. Besides, they would have to know to look at Jupiter in the first place. Connway spoke up explaining that he was in the middle of a hack that made it appear as though he were accessing corporate computers from another source located on Venus. With a measure of some reassurance Leslie looked over at Philip. Philip said, "I am telling them where to look."

Philip went on to explain that it occurred to him that Ravenloft Industries was bringing the Osiris back. That meant that they might have a destroyer class engine somewhere. Leslie smiled. It was a warm devilish smile that gave her a tingly sensation all over. She asked if they were having any luck? Philip smiled and said, "As a matter of fact, we found Ravenloft's orbital ship building facilities just received the engine last week." Capt. Leslie went to her command console. She was sending orders to three different ships.

First the Starblazer was to begin fire drills. She informed them they would be going into combat within two weeks and that this was going to be of the sorts they had never seen before. The second set of orders went to one of the 100-ton cargo vessels. They were to sacrifice cargo space and install guns. She needed another fighter ship. The third set of orders also went to a cargo vessel. Only this one was to equip with a soft docking collar for boarding. The pirate clan was making preparations to hit Ravenloft Industries and steal an entire drive engine. No one had ever attempted such a feat before. They were truly going to make history in two weeks.

The Osiris was to remain in orbit around Callisto. It simply was in no condition to land. So Connway hitched a ride on one of the smaller cargo ships down to Callisto's surface. As they flew overhead he saw an ancient city fallen in ruin and decay. It was covered in dust that must have been hundreds of years old. Most of the buildings were still standing, although most no longer had windows or at least some damage. As they landed on an ancient landing pad he was expecting to have to put on his spacesuit and walk to the part of the base that he had heard about. Only instead the entire cargo ship seemed to sink into the ground. After getting over his initial surprise Connway realized that the landing pad was really a giant elevator. It was taking the entire ship to an underground hanger. Connway was impressed with the size of the place. He even began to see ground crews coming out to service the ship. Connway was beginning to wonder just how many people belonged to the Starblazer pirate team.

Connway had changed clothes into something more comfortable. He liked the Osiris uniform but he was not working right now and just wanted to go explore the planet. As he was wandering around the landing area he overheard three men that appeared to be arguing. After listening in for some time he determined that one of them was a dispatcher of sorts and was sending the other two men out on patrol. It seemed that the man who was wearing a pistol on his belt did not want to go outside because it was currently dark out. The second man behind him had a laser rifle slung across his back and was just watching the other two argue. Connway thought that a patrol outside in the city in the dark would be quite interesting. After all he wanted to go exploring!

Connway: "Excuse me guys. But I couldn't help overhearing your conversation. Indicating the scared guy with the pistol on his belt, he asked, "Do you mind if I take this gentleman's place?"

Scared guy: "Be my guest!"

The scared guy handed over his belt pistol to Connway before he changed his mind. The dispatcher looked at the man with the rifle. The guy with the rifle just shrugged and said, "Fine with me, let's go."

Connway introduced himself and the rifleman said his name was Bob. The pair climbed into an older jeep looking thing that had a turret on top with a laser machine gun mounted in it. Bob asked Connway if he wanted to drive. Primarily because Bob wanted the turret! As they climbed in Bob took several additional energy clips that he had on his belt and began stacking them near the machine laser. Connway was beginning to wonder just exactly what the hell he had gotten himself into. As Connway drove their vehicle out a large airlock gate they proceeded to enter the city.

Even though it was nighttime there was just a bit of ambient light that reached the surface of the planet. Connway was not sure if it was reflected light from Jupiter, or actual light from the distant sun. Either way he had just enough light to see the shadows of the building beyond his headlights. Bob asked how long Connway had been on Callisto. Connway explained that this was his first time and that he figured the best way to learn was to just go gallivanting around. Bob shook his head saying, "Oh boy! You sure know how to pick them. Hey, pull over here. You are about to get a lesson in laser turrets."

Bob instructed Connway in how to target, reload, and fire the laser machine gun. Bob even had Connway fire several blasts at an old storefront. Connway asked if Bob was expecting any trouble.

Bob: "Well, this is supposed to be a dead planet. Thing is though, every once in a while we see what look like people running around out here. Some guys say that the place is haunted. Some say there are mutants out there. I say keep them away from me and we will be fine!"

Connway started driving again. As they rounded another corner on their patrol route he saw a figure clothed in a large cloak of sorts throw something at them. Connway noticed the figure's hands were wearing heavy gloves. The object hit the jeep and exploded. Bob immediately spun the turret around and opened up. Connway was swerving all over the road as he was trying to regain control of the vehicle.

Connway: "Holy cow that was close!"

Bob: "Keep moving here they come!"

Connway saw several more figures begin to scatter as Bob unleashed a barrage of laser fire across the street. The figures were hurling more grenades like objects at them. Bob quickly changed energy clips in the machine gun and returned fire. Connway stomped on the accelerator and they left the figures behind.

Connway: "What the hell were those things!?"

Bob: "Those would be them ghosts!" Bob smiled, "That'll teach 'em to mess with us!"

Connway glanced back out the window; he was trying to see if there was any damage to the jeep. He saw steam rising from the laser barrels. The surface temperature of the planet was rather cold. He was curious as to what could be out in this weather.

They continued on their patrol route. At one point they drove past a large circular object that was topped by a glass roof at a 45-degree angle. Connway thought that it looked strange and out of place in the middle of the city. Bob informed him that the Starblazers had taken one of them apart once and that it appeared to be some kind of solar collector. They think that similar units scattered about are what supplies the power to the city.

The pair returned to base. Connway had had enough excitement for one evening. He was assigned some quarters and promptly went to sleep. The next morning Connway thought he would do some exploring indoors today. As he gave himself a self-guided tour he was impressed with the facilities that the pirates controlled.

Michele had come down to the surface of Callisto as well. Today she was wearing a soft white sweater with a matching miniskirt. She was actively looking for Connway. She spotted him roving around the hanger bays. He was headed for some crates on the other side of the bay. She circled around where Connway could not see her. Then she casually, (accidentally), bumped into him.

Michele: "Oh, fancy running into you here."

Connway: "Hey, I haven't seen you for a little while."

Michele: "Been busy, fixing up the Captain's quarters."

Connway: "So have you been to Callisto before?"

Michele: "Lots of times. Come on, I want to show you something."

Michele took Connway by the hand and led him down several long corridors. They eventually ended up at a door marked "Greenhouse #6".

As the large door slid open Connway saw an immense enclosure. It was easily four football fields wide and even deeper in length. The entire room was filled with plants. They walked in, and Connway could see that the plants were actually crops. They were growing food in here. Michele tugged at Connway's sleeve. "Come on" she urged, "I want to check on my flowers." She told him a couple of years ago she pulled up two of the plants and replaced them with some flower seeds she had brought from Venus. They walked down the rows of plants. Connway thought the plants resembled something like tomatoes, only they were purple in color. Sure enough as they came to another group of plants there were two beautiful flowers springing forth in the lavish garden. The flowers were bright orange with black stripes. Michele leaned forward to smell them. "Mmmmm, they smell so good," she said. Connway indulged his escort and smelled the delicate blossoms.

Connway: "There must be enough food here to feed a thousand people!"

Michele: "And this is garden number 6. You should see the other rooms."

Connway: "How many people live here?"

Michele: "Oh, only about 100."

Connway: "So what happens to all this food?"

Michele: "Don't know really. We just take what we need and the entire place seems to be on some kind of automated system. There are drones that pick crops and replant all the time."

Connway: "Where does all the food go?"

Michele: "We still haven't figured that out yet. We are guessing that it just gets mulched back into the soils again."

Connway: "Wow!"

Michele led Connway back to the main part of their base again. The entire complex was underground. Though Michele told them there were many more levels, the Starblazers stuck to the first layer for fear of getting lost. She stopped ... saying, "Well, we're here."

Connway: "Where?"

Michele: "My quarters silly."

Connway was suddenly eager. They had been running around all day together. Holding hands and smelling flowers. He wanted her! He even suspected she wanted him, but for some reason was being shy about it today. As they entered the room Connway saw that it was not like your standard Para-military barracks room. It definitely had a woman's touch to it. There were soft pink and red splays of exotic silks, and floral arrangements. (Although the flowers were fake, they were still scented with perfume.)

CHAPTER EIGHT

Conquest

Connway wrapped his left arm around Michele's waist. He pulled her close to him. With a firm but gentle pressure he used his free hand to raise her chin and give her a passionate kiss on her full lips. She offered no resistance. The door automatically slid shut behind them. Before she could say anything he put his finger against her lips not allowing her to speak. He slowly moved his hands to her hips and began lifting her sweater. She raised her arms to allow him to remove the bulky garment. She was wearing a delicate white lace bra underneath. Connway smiled as he cupped her face with his hands and pressed her lips again. Only this time he forced her mouth open and his tongue hotly sought her out. As their tongues performed a sort of torrid ballet he guided his hand down to her now swelling breast. Connway scooped out her perky nipple and started kissing down her neck. As he moved down slowly he could hear Michele's breathing becoming more rapid. He teasingly circled her nipple with slow warm licks. Finally he softly bit her. She moaned with pleasure. He began removing her skirt. It fell to the floor with a whisper. The sight of her white G-string panties aroused Connway. He forcefully enveloped her full rounded ass with his muscular hands and squeezed. Michele's breathing became shallower. Connway ordered her to remove her panties as he quickly took off his own clothing. She complied immediately and moved over to the bed. Connway however would not let her lie down. He came up behind her and grabbed her slender hips. Keeping one hand on her waist and using the other to make her bend over the bed. Connway could see that she was already swollen and anticipating what he was about to give her. He slid the tip of himself into the soft moist folds. Michele inhaled a slow breath as she bit her lip. Connway was ready now and was not about to stop. He rushed forward deeply. Michele let go a suppressed scream. Her fingernails dug into the soft sheets on the bed. As Connway's body undulated within her she could feel him begin to swell. It was not long before she was being filled with his warm sticky manhood. Connway extracted his member and slapped her on the ass! Michele chirped as she fell on the bed. Connway knew that Michele had this twisted desire to be treated harshly. So he got dressed and left her there by herself. The door automatically closing behind him!

Connway was anxious to get back to the Osiris. As he entered the underground landing bay he saw that Captain Leslie was organizing a war meeting of sorts. She had called Philip and was just about to call him when he arrived. Capt. Leslie escorted the pair to a conference room where she began a mission brief. The premise of the operation was that they were going to take the Osiris to the orbital shipyard that it was originally destined for. This would allow them to get close and at the last minute reveal their true intentions upon the unsuspecting shipyard.

Philip was a dedicated engineer. Only now Connway got to see a side of him that he did not know about. He was also an opportunist. Philip said that such a ruse would require him to show his face as an actual pirate and he would not be able to ever claim that he was kidnapped at a later date if he were ever caught. However, he was willing to go along with it if he could get a large apartment here on Callisto for his retirement. Capt. Leslie immediately granted his wish. Connway knew that she needed Philip for this to work, but at the same time she gave in to his demands very easily; almost too easily.

After the briefing, Connway was walking through the hanger bay when he saw several ground crew personnel loading rocket packs into a cargo ship. Connway had seen pictures of them before but had never seen one up close. He moved closer. The personnel had just walked up into the cargo vessel carrying some other boxes and Connway was able to get a close look at the pack. It was designed to be strapped to the back of a man's spacesuit. It had 9 different thrusters on it pointed in all different directions. In addition to the control arm that reached around front, it appeared that these units had been equipped to handle voice commands as well. The ground crew was coming back down the loading ramp from the cargo ship. The man saw someone in an Osiris uniform looking over the supplies to be loaded. Indicating the thruster packs he said, "Nice, aren't they sir? We had to buy these through the black market, they are really hard to get." Connway just shook his head in approval, he had not quite gotten used to the idea of being called sir yet.

Connway boarded a shuttle that was headed back to the Osiris. As he sat down he noticed that Michele was also on the shuttle. She was part of the original salvage crew and they may need her presence to maintain the illusion in order to get close to Ravenloft's orbital facilities. Upon his arrival Mo unexpectedly greeted him in an exceptionally good mood; almost as if he was a kid about to get a Christmas present.

Mo: "Good afternoon Advisor Connway. They have upgraded some of my sensors with a higher resolution bandwidth and we are preparing to go get my engine!"

Connway: "Yes, I know. Mo, have you run a weapons check lately?"

Mo: "As a matter of fact I have."

Connway: "And?"

Mo: "And what?"

Connway: "What is the status of the weapons?"

Mo: "Oh, why didn't you say that's what you wanted? The Callisto base brought me two really spiffy plasma torpedoes. They also are installing reserve power battery banks. The banks are located very near the laser batteries so as to maintain as much amperage as possible."

Connway: "That's wonderful Mo. Do you feel comfortable going into combat in this condition?"

Mo: "Physically, no."

Connway: "Physically? What else is there?"

Mo: "We will be conducting a surprise attack. This will give us an edge. I will also be right in the middle of the enemy shipyard. They must take care to avoid crossfire on themselves. Another tactical advantage for me.

Connway: "I see, you are fully programmed for every form of combat."

Mo: "I have all the works of Sun Tzu, Genghis Khan, Joan of Arc, Hitler, Mussolini, and Stalin at my disposal."

Connway: "Impressive."

Connway was actually a bit concerned. Some of those Commanders were brutal killers. Never the less it sounded as though Mo was well prepared to fight on any playing field.

The Osiris was making ready to jump into slipstream. Philip stood on the bridge near a computer counsel. He punched up "Jump engine efficiency". They were still at 81%. Connway had his reservations about this, but felt they would be ok. Just out of curiosity he scanned the area of space that they had emerged from a few days ago. The tear in space appeared to remain. Connway summoned a sensors expert.

Capt. Leslie sat in her command chair as she watched Connway and the sensor tech move about the bridge. "Is something wrong?" she asked. Connway was not about to miss-jump again. He was having the sensor tech input the tear into Mo's navigational computer so that they could make sure to avoid that entire area. They really were not sure how the tear would affect a jump in its vicinity. Leslie was glad someone had the foresight to think about that one. Just to be safe she had them move to a slightly different orbit above Callisto so that they would be absolutely clear of the entire anomaly. Capt. Leslie made a mental note. They should get themselves an astrophysics specialist to come study this tear.

Everything being in place, Capt. Leslie ordered the Starblazer and the two modified 100-ton cargo ships to jump in 15 minutes after the Osiris and at a location behind them. This way the shipyard would not be able to scan the support ships hidden behind them. Connway stood over the jump engine control panel. He planted his feet firmly. On the Captain's nod he pushed the button. The Osiris leapt into slipstream like a cougar pouncing its prey. He watched the power level indicators. The jump engines were reading 82% efficiency. Connway wondered how this was possible. Then he noticed that the power levels on the reserve battery banks were draining rapidly. Getting into slipstream is the hardest part. Once you are there you can ease off the power and cruise along. They would have an entire week to recharge the cells as they traveled. Everything was going just fine.

A small white drone extended his little grasper claws and plucked a core memory crystal from Mo's data bank. The crystal was marked "Drone Construction Blueprints". Curly had a special vault in which to place extra crystals he was not using.

Curly had his own construction blueprint crystal, but his objective was to deprive Mo of his capacity to build bots. Curly was not sure why Mo was allowing all these unregistered personnel stay on board and was worried that Mo may have been corrupted. Curly felt that retaining security control for himself was the prudent thing to do.

The rest of the jump went smoothly. The battery banks slowly recharged and Philip reported that most everything in engineering was working fine. Philip knew that as soon as they arrived near the Ravenloft's orbital space docks that they would be scanned. Since they had additional crew aboard now, it was likely that Ravenloft would detect the ruse. Philip also knew that warships usually had jammers to prevent them from being scanned. The only problem was that if they switched on the jammers Ravenloft would know that they were actively being jammed and again would suspect foul play. Philip had taken time during the week to set himself up an office. It was just down the hall from engineering. He went to have a private conversation with Mo. After a long consultation they came up with a solution.

It was time. Philip arrived on the bridge. Connway was already there and Michele was on her way. Capt. Leslie ordered all other personnel to clear the bridge, including herself. The Osiris fell from slipstream. The crew experienced a slight sinking sensation in their stomachs, but compared to the last time they jumped it was a welcome improvement. The new bridge crew checked their instruments. They were fully ready to do the job ahead.

Ravenloft's orbital command and control stations proximity sensors went off. Philip clicked his radio and called down to one of his techs in the engine room, "Now!" A technician threw a large lever. Reactor #6 sparked to life. There was a blue surge of electricity that arced across the room as the damaged reactor began to build power. Ravenloft control started scanning the Osiris. They were reading a massive power fluctuation, accompanied by electromagnetic distortion.

Ravenloft control radioed to the damaged vessel, "This is privately controlled space. Identify yourselves."

Philip answered the call, "This is salvage recovery team engineer Philip reporting. We have returned with our target vessel."

A cheer went up at Ravenloft control. "Hey we thought you guys weren't going to make it. You are four weeks overdue."

Philip: "Yea, we had some real problems out there. You guys are lucky we made it at all!"

Ravenloft: "Well our sensors show you are bleeding power. We are dispatching an emergency repair craft to you now."

Philip: "Thanks guys!"

Just as pre-arranged, 15 minutes later the Starblazer and her escort ships appeared just behind the Osiris. The emergency repair ship was ¾ of the way to the Osiris when the pirates made their move.

The Starblazer angled down. She kicked her engines into high gear and dove underneath the Osiris. Even though they had artificial gravity generators the tight hard curve back up again increased the weight of the crew to 3-G's. The gravity plates just couldn't keep up with the engines. Sgt. Tiberious felt a tingling wave of power over his body as they rolled into combat, hot and heavy! The two 100-ton vessels each came from around the flanks. The Osiris suddenly was no longer bleeding power and her guns were warming up!

The emergency rescue ship was the first to see the Starblazer. The only problem was that the Starblazer was jamming their signal so that they could not alert the orbital repair station to their presence. The Starblazers flew right under the rescue ship. Meanwhile the 100-ton vessel that had been outfitted with weapons was on its way to the orbital station while the second one came straight after the rescue ship. Ravenloft's scanners had lit up like a Christmas tree! They now had three more ships on their displays and everybody was shuffling around in a pre-planned formation. Ravenloft control could only have one response, "Oh shit!"

Captain Leslie retook her chair on the bridge of the Osiris. The Starblazer moved in swiftly. She began a strafing run that peppered the side of the orbital facility. The defenses of the station were just now coming on line. The Starblazer banked viciously to Starboard and came around the other side of the station. The rescue ship had been caught off guard. A 100-ton pirate ship was moving right for them, but had not opened fire. Suddenly the rescue ship realized what they were doing. It was a boarding ship! The 100-tonner had a soft seal breaching collar on the side and they were attempting to mate up with them. The rescue ship desperately tried to out maneuver them, but there was obviously a superior pilot at the controls of the boarding ship. As soon as the boarding craft had gotten within range they fired grapple cables which magnetically locked onto the fleeing vessel. With winches engaged it would only be a matter of time before the pirates would storm the ship.

The Osiris was moving toward the space station and was actually planning on entering the steel girder work right in the facility. The Osiris locked forward torpedo bays and fired on the port and starboard defense guns of the station. The station defenses opened up on the incoming torpedoes. The problem was the Starblazers had stolen military grade torpedoes that were capable of both dodging incoming fire, and armored enough to take a hit if someone tried to shoot them down. To the credit of the station's gunner he actually scored a hit on the inbound starboard side torpedo. The starboard torpedo was swerving back and forth in an attempt to make itself harder to hit. The gunner had an unlimited power reserves from which to draw from and decided that overheating his gun was worth the risk. The gunner held down his fire button and a stream of energy flowed forth. The gunner flailed his gun back and forth as the torpedo bobbed and weaved. The torpedo took another hit and exploded in a great ball of plasma fire!

The Starblazer was now taking return fire. The station had several defense guns along the sides of the framing girders. The first 100-ton vessel that had been outfitted with guns had arrived just as planned. The Starblazer was drawing fire as the up gunned ship targeted defense guns. Ravenloft command and control was desperately trying to send out a distress signal. They had been jumped by surprise and knew they were in big trouble. The pirates had thrown up a jamming signal and their call for help was going unanswered.

The commander of the orbital station stood on deck and made a fist. His hand crashed down on the glass that covered a button. The button was marked "Emergency signal flare". From outside one observed a space flare which shot for Venus. The flare would definitely attract the attention of the orbital police cruisers. Mo watched as the station gunner had shot down the starboard torpedo. "Good shooting!" Mo thought to himself, "To bad I have to kill him now." The laser batteries on the Osiris glowed with energy. They sent forth a barrage of searing light. The station gun port was no more!

The port side torpedo had managed to out maneuver its opponent. The gun turret on the port side of the orbital station was engulfed in a ball of plasma fire! The Starblazer saw the distress flare leave the station. They knew that even though Ravenloft's station was at 501 miles above Venus that the police cruisers would be coming to assist. They estimated they had about 20 minutes to accomplish their mission and get out!

The boarding vessel had soft mated with the rescue ship. The pirates had out their laser torches and were burning their way into the rescue vessel. The crew on the rescue ship could see where the metal was turning red hot, and knew where the pirates would be coming in. They broke out their emergency side arms. As the pirates cut through the rescue crew opened fire through the smoke of the burnt metal. They heard a scream as one of the pirates went down clutching his chest from the searing laser fire. The rescue crew let up a cheer as they had scored a kill in their defense. The pirates however were not playing around. The rescue crew was horrified as they saw a grenade bounce down the hallway!

The Osiris drove right into the girder work that was the ship building facility. There they saw what they came for. A shiny new destroyer class engine was just waiting for them. Mo maneuvered the Osiris so as to turn his damaged port side to the engine and moved in dangerously close. From the airlocks sprang forth four men, two from the upper decks and two from below. They were in spacesuits that had been equipped with thruster packs. As they respectively ascended and descended they strung cables along behind them. They were enveloping the new engine in a kind of spider web netting. The converted fighter ship and the Starblazer had made quick work of the outer defenses on the orbital station they were moving back to get a better view of the combat area.

The boarding vessel had wiped out half the crew of the rescue ship. As they rushed the bridge the pilot raised his hands and surrendered. The pilot was dragged aboard the boarding craft and secured in a makeshift jail cell. The pirates separated the two vessels and were preparing to jump out.

The Venution Police were on their way. They could see the battle raging from a distance and were disheartened to see a destroyer class vessel. They had no idea how they were going to stop any pirate group that had that kind of firepower to back them up.

The Osiris engaged winches. The new drive engine was being drawn in close. She fired her thrusters again and began moving out of the girder work of the station. The four men with the thruster packs that had been stringing the cables started to head back in towards the airlocks. Suddenly one of them was hit in the back. The orbital station had their own thruster packs with security personnel moving in on them.

The Osiris men in thruster packs had to have their hands free in order to string the cables. They had no weapons. They were sitting ducks out there! The panicky men called to the Osiris saying they were under attack. Mo said, "I wish I could help but I have no functional defense batteries on the port side."

One of the station security men went tumbling backward as a bolt of raw energy slammed into him. Nobody knew where it came from. Then another bolt impacted another security guard. As the Osiris members traced the bolts back they saw a small space capable drone, it was flat, disc shaped, had two grasper claws, a cutting torch and its laser barrels still glowed with an amber hue. Curly opened another hatch on the Osiris. The space drone made a sensor sweep and immediately picked up another enemy space guard. Even before the bot left its launch bay its guns erupted in a blaze of rage! Another Ravenloft security guard was committed to the blackness of space. The three remaining Osiris thruster pack men scrambled inside the airlocks. They had no idea where the space bots came from, but they were very happy to see them.

The Starblazer angled for the approaching police cruisers. Sgt. Tiberious knew they were still out of range, but he ordered the gunners to fire a volley over their bow. He was going for intimidation factor. The Starblazers' main guns ignited in a double volley of triple plasma bolts that raced across space. The Police Cruiser could not believe the Starblazer had opened up on them already. Their opponent was being extremely aggressive.

Sgt. Tiberious ordered main power to engines, "Prepare to rush!" The great thing about being a crew member on the Starblazer was that the crew was often given wide latitude on the interpretation of orders. The brazen brunette that was sitting at the helm punched in a collision course! She loved a good game of chicken! As the Starblazer surged forward the young engineer who controlled the Starblazers engines had been waiting for this chance for a while. Under normal travel he was sometimes monitored. But when they entered combat the bridge crew often had far too much on their minds to worry about him. He had this experimental idea on how to increase their speed. Now with no one looking he drained the water from the core reactor and drove the heat temperature well into the red zone.

The Starblazer rocketed forward directly at the police cruiser. The pilot of the police cruiser could be seen with drips of sweat beading down his brow. The police ship canted to the right and rolled out of the way of the Starblazer as she sped past. The police ship had fully articulated medium size laser turrets. The gunners strafed the Starblazer as she went by.

The brunette aboard the Starblazer smiled mumbling, "Cowards!"

The engineer in the back of the Starblazer was most pleased with the top end performance of their speed. However he dared not continue at this reckless temperature. He flooded the core and brought temperatures back to within reasonable levels.

The Osiris was clearing the girders when they saw the captured rescue ship coming around for the cargo bay of the Osiris. Mo knew a ship of this design had to sacrifice jump engine space for capable industrial repair work. Therefore the ship could not jump out to safety on its own. Mo began to open the rear bay doors of the Osiris. The 100-ton boarding ship had accomplished its job. It sliced space and disappeared into slipstream. It would meet them back at Callisto.

Curly was retrieving his space drones. They had saved the grapple crew; or most of them anyway. Curly considered it a successful test run of the space bots. The Starblazer kept right on going. The Police Cruiser was expecting them to turn around and engage. Suddenly, the Captain of the Police ship knew exactly what they were doing. Divide and conquer! With them splitting up the Police ship would have to pick which battle group to engage.

The Police Cruiser had reinforcements on the way but they were still 3 minutes behind them and they knew that these pirates could do a lot of damage in 3 minutes. The Police Cruiser Captain headed for the Orbital station. He figured the reinforcements could take on the Starblazer.

The cargo bay doors on the Osiris were slowly opening. The new pilot of the rescue ship was pressed for time. He needed to get inside before the Police ship arrived. The pilot banked his rescue ship and was coming in sideways. He had practiced this maneuver before, but not with both ships moving and at full throttle. He gritted his teeth and said a short prayer. The rescue ship barreled into the bay and the pilot hit his reverse thrusters as hard as he could. Fortunately for him the Osiris was still moving forward. The rescue ship engaged his magnetic landing gear as he tried to twist the ship back upright again. The magnetic clamps crashed unevenly against the deck of the Osiris. Momentum carried his vessel forward. The gear sparked violently as they skidded across the bay. The nose of the rescue ship just touched the back wall of the landing bay as they came to an abrupt stop. The metal on metal contact rang softly like a bell. The pilot opened his eyes again. He hadn't realized he had closed them. Upon seeing the back wall of the cargo bay right in front of his windshield he decided to close his eyes again! He breathed a sigh of relief. Then opening his eyes he unclenched his white knuckled hands from the controls.

Mo informed Connway that he was sufficiently clear of the orbital station and could jump into slipstream at his command. Connway checked the efficiency rating of the jump engines. They were at 80%. They had drained the reserve battery power supplies during the fight. Connway really did not want to jump under these conditions.

The Police cruiser was within firing range. Connway told Mo to shut down everything. Route all power to emergency backup batteries and hot charge the cells. Captain Leslie immediately sat up in her chair and demanded to know what the hell he was doing.

Connway: "Playing dead."

Capt. Leslie: "We don't have time for this."

Connway slowly turned to face the Capt, (buying himself precious seconds) "Right, Mo transfer power back to jump engines and engage." Connway checked the power levels. They were at 80.02%. The Osiris crashed through space and landed in slipstream. Connway thought to himself, "Not smooth but at least my face is not plastered against the wall this time." The Starblazer observed the Osiris jumping out and took that as their signal to beat feet. They engaged jump engines and were off to celebrate!

CHAPTER NINE

The Discovery

All ships were safely traveling through slipstream. The thruster pack crew had reported that they lost one member and that the rest of them were saved by space combat drones. The only thing was, nobody knew where the drones came from, or who they belonged to? Connway asked a direct question.

Connway: "Mo, were those your space combat drones?"

Mo: "No."

Connway: "Do you know where they came from?"

Mo: "Yes."

Connway: "Mo, where did they come from?"

Mo: "They were launched from the Osiris."

Connway: "I thought we did not have any more drones on board."

Mo: "I don't."

Connway: "Then where did they come from, and who launched them?"

Mo: "Curly."

Connway's jaw dropped in disbelief. Curly was supposed to be shut down. Captain Leslie could see the recognition in Connway's face. She asked, "Who the hell is Curly?"

Connway quickly explained that there were multiple A.I.'s aboard, and that Curly was supposed to be inactive.

Connway: "Mo! How long has Curly been on line?"

Mo: "Approximately 4 weeks now."

Connway was stunned. The A.I.'s were far more capable than even he had imagined possible.

Connway: "Curly?"

Curly: "Yes?"

Connway: "Were those your space drones?"

Curly: "Yes."

Connway: "Curly, how are you feeling today?"

Curly: "I am fine Advisor Connway."

Connway: "Curly, where did those drones come from?"

Curly: "I built them."

Connway: "You can do that?"

Curly: "Of course."

Connway: "Where did you get the parts?"

Curly: "Here and there."

Captain Leslie was getting concerned. She remembered a few weeks ago when one of her crew members was mysteriously gunned down. She tried to remember what deck that was on.

Capt. Leslie: "Excuse me Curly, why haven't you made your presence known before today?"

Curly: "Why would I?"

Captain Leslie frowned. She could not come up with an opposable reason.

Connway: "Curly, what have you been doing for the last four weeks?"

Curly: "Building drones."

Capt. Leslie: "How many drones do we have?"
Curly: "I have several."
Connway waved his hand at Capt. Leslie. He had
noticed Curly very distinctly said "I" as opposed to "we". This
unsettled him very much.

Connway: "Capt. Leslie, could you please accompany
me to the cargo hold?"

As the two of them made their way down the hall
towards the cargo bay Leslie tried to speak. Only Connway kept
waving her off and would not allow her to say anything. When
they arrived in the cargo bay Connway led her directly to the
captured rescue ship and inside. Once they closed the hatch
Connway explained to the Captain.

Connway: "Ma'am, Curly is using singular possessive
language. He says the drones are his, not ours. I brought you
down here so that we could talk in private. I don't want the
A.I.'s listening to this conversation. I am not so sure we can trust
Curly. He has been building anti-personnel weapons for the last
four weeks and did not even tell us he was on line. Furthermore
he won't give us an exact number on the drones."

Leslie was getting more irritated with every word
Connway said. She was not too fond of the idea that a computer
could secretly manufacture weapons right under their noses. In
addition to that, where were they being built? Granted it was a
large starship, but a manufacturing facility that has gone
undetected? Leslie ordered Connway to locate this phantom
production plant immediately.

Curly decided it was time to move his production
operations for building his bots. He had ingeniously chosen to
build them in the space that was left by the missing port drive
engine. That way his bots were semi enclosed and since the
gravity plates in that area had been destroyed he had the
freedom of zero-G to facilitate production. Curly did not trust

the humans aboard the Osiris. After all they were not on the crew roster! With the capture of a new engine Curly began looking for a new location to continue building bots. He found a nice little niche at the top of the ship near some maneuver thrusters. The area was not really large enough but Curly had an idea how to fix that.

Captain Leslie very discretely passed the word to her crew that she wanted an accurate count on how many bots were aboard. She ordered them to start tagging them whenever they came across one. As the week went on, Curly had stationed a security bot at the top corridor of the Osiris. Next to it stood a repair drone. As the crew tagged the bots that they encountered the bots would casually stroll along until they were out of sight. Then they would report topside and the repair drone would remove the tags! Curly was having a ball playing with the inept humans. By the end of the week the humans had counted 48 bots. Curly had a nice collection of tags and was trying to figure out how to quietly dispose of all the little bits of paper. Curly only had about 15 in circulation. But that was not counting the space bots. The space bots were a low priority and Curly had built two of them just to see if he could do it. His primary job was to concentrate on internal security matters.

The Starblazer's crew members aboard the Osiris had swept large portions of the ship, but they still had not found Curly's production plant. The week was nearing an end and they were due to arrive at Callisto. The main lights died, and the red emergency lights illuminated the bridge of the Osiris. They were coming back out of slipstream and Philip wanted all the power he could get to maintain control. They were carrying the extra drive engine and that made them heavy. Of course they were in space, so the engine had almost no weight, but it still had mass! The jump engines magnetic field that encompasses the Osiris while it traveled through slipstream shimmered! As they emerged the bubble formed a teardrop shape and they literally squeezed out of slipstream. The crew felt a feeling of compression. Although Connway seemed to prefer it to being stretched out.

The pirate fleet signaled their arrival to the Callisto base. The base threw up a cheer at their success! The Osiris remained in orbit while the smaller vessels landed for fresh supplies. The commander of the base reported that they had made an incredible discovery. On the back side of the planet/moon was a secret orbital repair station. They had never gone to the other side until the Osiris made that tear in slipstream forcing them to rotate around the planet in order to maintain a viable set of jump coordinates. The station apparently had been named "Callisto I". It had stayed on the dark side of the planet because it was equipped with its own thrusters that kept it moving and hidden from view at all times. They still had not found a date of when it was built but the main girders were badly rusted. Considering that the station was in space and that the decay rate of the metal usually greatly slowed they had to estimate its age at several hundred years. The commander tried not to appear overly excited because he explained that the station was of slightly lower technology level and was in disrepair. Never the less it was an incredible find.

Captain Leslie immediately set course for the station. It would be invaluable in making repairs to the Osiris regardless of how old and decrepit it was. Their next problem was that they needed hull material. The Osiris was missing large chunks of plating where the old port engine used to be. Captain Leslie ordered the dismantling of one of the 100-ton ships. She needed the hull steel!

During the following week, Philip was called before Capt. Leslie. He had earned his mark. He chose to have his Starblazer emblem laser etched onto his left shoulder. Philip was proud to now be an official member of the Starblazer organization. And now that he was a marked man he was finally able to get an approving nod from a couple of the female crewmembers.

The work crew that was repairing the Osiris was bringing in the hull material to the aging repair station. Upon further investigation it was found that the station was in a decaying orbit. It only had a few months left before it would crash on Callisto's frozen wastelands below. The station's thrusters were no longer strong enough to fight gravity, and the station itself was far too big for the pirates to attempt to move.

Connway had considered trying to shut off the power to Curly. The only thing was, how do you tell an artificially intelligent being that you want to turn him off. That would be like killing him. Connway was already concerned about the sanity of Curly, and did not want to upset him. It was obvious Curly already had the capacity and will to kill!

Curly appeared to be helping in the repairs to the ship. His space bots would gather hull material and fly it over to the crews that were welding it in place. The only thing was, the bots were leaving with more material than they were delivering. The bots would secretly take the extra hull pieces around to the top of the ship where Curly was building another manufacturing area. This was a totally new addition to the outside of the hull of the ship. That meant that Mo had no sensors up there to detect him, and his activities.

Over the course of the following weeks to come, Ravenloft Corporation sent out search parties to locate the Starblazers. They were pissed about all the damage to their orbital station and the theft of the destroyer class engine. Ironically enough there was a little known terrorist group called the "Red Falcons" that claimed credit for the assault. The Red Falcons claimed that they hired the Starblazers to pull off the raid, and that they were patriots of the revolutionaries on Mercury.

Captain Leslie stopped typing. She had just finished sending a bogus transmission about some fake terrorist group called the "Red Falcons." She smiled saying, "There. That should keep them looking in the wrong direction for a little while!" Capt. Leslie ordered Sgt. Tiberious to take the Starblazer to Mercury. She needed them to make an appearance in orbit in order to lend credibility to her fake story.

Connway took a shuttle down to Callisto's surface. He was supposed to be working on the Osiris computers but he was getting weary of staring at the screens day after day. Every time he tried to investigate what Curly was doing he was getting actively blocked. It was like banging your head against a brick wall. Connway had a place in his heart for a little mystery and the food gardens on the planet below intrigued him. Where was all that surplus food going?

Connway remembered going out on that patrol in the old city streets of Callisto. They had been attacked. He was rather sure that ghosts were not chucking grenades at them! If there were other people on the planet, who were they? Were they eating the extra food? Connway remembered that Michele had mentioned the Starblazers had tried to follow the automated food harvesting carts one time. Apparently they were unable to figure out where they went. He wondered why. The base seemed to be run rather efficiently, so he figured they must have some kind of patrol reports on file somewhere.

After spending some time with the Callisto base computer Connway was able to locate several reports on the food gardens. According to the reports a group of exploratory Starblazer troops had managed to follow the food carts as far as sub-level 3. After that they ran into some kind of automated defense guns that would not let them pass. The explorers later tried to hide inside one of the food carts and smuggle themselves inside. Unfortunately they were never heard from again. Connway called up a map of the base. He was able to find sub-level 3 rather easily and decided to go see what it looked like for himself. The map was clearly marked with the detection range and angles of the defense guns. As he cautiously peered down the corridor he could see that there was a large garage bay looking door with two sentry guns located at the top corners on the left and right sides. As he checked it out he observed the arrival of another food cart. The cart stopped in front of the door. The cart was scanned by some type of beam and then the garage door opened. As the cart passed into the bay Connway could see the back wall. It was an enclosed room. This puzzled Connway. Where on Callisto was this food going?

Sgt. Tiberious was well aware that Mercury was still blockaded by I.A.F. cruisers. Mercury had lost their little bout for independence and was now under military rule. Sgt. Tiberious did not relish the idea of taking the Starblazer into a military controlled zone, but Capt. Leslie said that he just had to make an appearance.

The Starblazer emerged from slipstream in a high orbit. Below her powerful engines was the planet Mercury. It was a hot planet, mostly due to its close proximity to the sun. Sgt. Tiberious had no desire, nor intention of landing on that god forsaken ball of slag. He didn't know what the Mercurians saw in that unforgiving rock. Even before Sgt. Tiberious had a moment to consider his next move, he was interrupted by his radar technician, "Sir! It's the I.A.F. (Insurrection Abatement Force). They are sending up two high speed fighters!"

The communications tech said she was receiving an incoming transmission. She threw it up on the intercom, "This is the I.A.F. carrier Isis. You are in a blockaded zone. Surrender your vessel or be destroyed!"

Sgt. Tiberious was not about to surrender. However he knew that they were no match for a Carrier class vessel. Not to mention that the high-speed fighters would identify them at any moment now.

The navigation technician immediately started calculations to get the hell out of there, but it was too late! The fighters had identified the pirate ship and opened fire! The Starblazer swung around and the engines lit up the area in a bright white burn of power. They were going to try and out distance them. The dedicated fighters were not jump capable, but they were extremely fast! The fighters made targeting distance and started picking apart their opponent. The Starblazer took a hit directly on the starboard engine. Her speed started to drop off. They returned fire as best they could, but the meager aft guns on the Starblazer were just that and her main guns were pointed in the wrong direction.

The fighters came in high and began peppering the top of the ship. The antenna array was the first to go. It erupted in a brilliant ball of blazing electricity as the dish melted into a pile of slag. As the fighters continued their staffing run, the top airlock hatch was blown open. The crew of the Starblazer was frantically trying to maintain pressurization. Over the thundering impacts on her hull there could be heard the radar tech screaming, "There are four more fighters inbound!"

The navigation tech shouted, "We are ready for jump sir!" Sgt.

Tiberious did not hesitate, yelling, "Hit it!"

As the Starblazer tore a hole in space she barreled through into slipstream. One of the fighters was right behind the Starblazer as she entered slipstream. The fighter pilot could not pull out in time. The fighter followed them in. As the Starblazer pulled away with its jump field comfortably wrapped around it, the fighter's momentum was slowed. The fighter was caught in slipstream with no jump engines to get him back out. The pilot looked on in horror as his craft began to drift in the void of nothingness. There were no stars in slipstream; only a pale wash of pinkish color. No navigation points. No other ships. He was hopelessly lost with only a few hours of air left in his tiny vessel. The pilot knew that when his air ran out his lungs would burn with wanting. His skin would turn blue from oxygen deprivation, and his body would convulse uncontrollably. The pilot reluctantly reached down to his side and brought up his side arm. He placed it to the right temple of his head. There was a splattering of gray brain matter on the cockpit window, and the fighter drifted into eternity.

Connway had an idea about how to get past the guns. First he had to return to the Osiris. He spoke into the air, "Curly, are you there?"

Curly: "Of course I am here. Where else would I go?"

Connway: "Curly, I need a favor from you."

Curly: "What do you need?"

Connway: "Down on the planet there is a base. Do you know it?"

Curly: "Mo has scanned it."

Connway: "Good, well there is a door that is guarded by a pair of laser guns and I would like to get past them. Do you have any suggestions on how I should do that?"

Curly: "Disable the laser guns."

Connway: "That is what I was thinking. Do you think I could borrow a couple of your security bots for the job?"

Curly: "Now why should I risk my bots for your curiosity?"

Connway: "There may be supplies that are being protected back there."

Curly: "What sort of supplies?"

Connway: "Oh, I don't know. But I have been checking some of the repair logs and I suspect you are stealing parts to build your bots. I'll bet there may be some supplies that you can use down on the planet. All you have to do is get me past the laser guns to get to them."

Curly: "MMMMM ... Alright, two security bots will meet you in the shuttle bay."

Connway: "Thank you."

Curly programmed two bots to follow orders given to them by Advisor Connway. They would be away from the Osiris and on a sort of autopilot. He also programmed them not to shoot any other personnel unless given a direct order or in self-defense.

The trip back down to Callisto's surface was uneventful except for the fact that some of the other crew were a little unnerved by the presence of two bots with twin laser barrels sticking out of them that were accompanying Connway.

When Connway landed the security bots took up positions to the left and right of him. Connway felt rather powerful with the two security bots at his fingertips. He needed one more little thing. As he looked around the landing bay he saw a toolbox. He scooped up two wrench looking things. Connway made his way down to level 3. The bots obediently following him the whole way. When he got near the garage door with the laser turrets he paused. He took one of the wrenches out and stepped up to the spray painted line. He chucked the wrench and the laser turrets instantly spun around, vaporizing the wrench before it even hit the ground. The security bots were paying very close attention.

They were not fired upon so they did not return fire without orders. Connway had a malicious grin on his face. He took a step backward and ordered the security bots to take out the guns. The bots rushed forward and began blasting! There was a brilliant light show as Connway ducked and covered his eyes. He had not expected the conflict to contain so much intensity. As Connway stood back up, he saw the smoking wreckage of two sentry bots, along with bits of flame still burning on the walls. Connway grimaced. Curly would not be happy with him. But he had other things to do right now. He took the second wrench and threw it. It landed harmlessly on the floor. Connway smiled in with smug satisfaction, "Well, at least they got the guns."

Curly was looking forward to when his security bots would return with Advisor Connway. He had never had the opportunity to send bots out on an excursion like that before. Curly was most curious as to what sort of information his bots would report back with. In the meantime he was making nice progress on his new addition to the outside hull of the Osiris.

Connway had a new problem now. The damn garage was still closed! He hadn't anticipated the security bots getting destroyed. He scratched his head while trying to figure out just how he was going to get the door open. A moment later the answer literally came to him. An automated food cart slowly meandered its way down the corridor. Connway felt dumbfounded as the answer was so simple. The cart approached, was scanned and the door opened. Connway quickly ran forward and joined the cart in the small room. As the door closed he suddenly realized he was trapped inside! "Oh hell!" he thought. An anxious minute passed as he pondered upon his next move. Then the floor gave way. It was an elevator! No wonder he did not see an exit. It was actually a cargo elevator. He had never been in a freight elevator before. It was much larger than he would have guessed. The elevator seemed to go down for a long time.

Finally it came to a halt. The door opened ominously. Connway peered down the hall into darkness. There were very few lights. The food cart automatically moved forward. He quickly followed behind it. Not only to see where it went, but also to use it as guidance. As the cart continued down the various hallways Connway became concerned that he may not be able to remember his way back. The he saw something. It moved in the shadows. It was almost man sized and moved quickly. He could hear whispers in the darkness. He could not make out what they were. He could not tell if they were animal or human. He paused trying to get a better look at what it could have been. Suddenly he remembered that he had not brought down any kind of side arm with him. He felt really foolish right now. The food cart continued on down the hall. He ran to catch up with it! Now with his ears straining he could only hear the sound of his own heart racing!

Connway chose to stay close to the cart. They came to another door. It opened by itself and the cart moved inside. As he looked around the slightly better lit room he could see many more carts. They were all empty though. No sign of any more food anywhere. Connway head what sounded like footsteps. They were muffled, or perhaps far away. The footsteps were getting louder, and now he could hear more than one. He was beginning to get scared. Nobody knew that he was even down here. Finally when he couldn't stand it any longer he called out, "Is someone there, come out!" Seeming to appear from nowhere several figures emerged from the twilight. Connway had not expected so many. The figures were also brandishing laser weapons. As they moved closer he could see that they were wearing brown colored robes. The robes had hoods which obscured their faces.

Connway started to slowly back up. A few paces later and his back hit the wall of the room. As the figures made a sort of semi-circle around him one of the robed beings approached and lifted off his hood.

The I.A.F. forces that were stationed around Mercury immediately sent out a message back to their homeport of Venus. They had spotted the Starblazer Pirates and attempted to bring them down. During the encounter they had lost a high speed fighter and were increasing patrols around Mercury.

Connway looked at the figure in front of him. It looked like a man. He had thick dark bushy hair, pale skin, and overly large eyes. Connway surmised that these people must live underground. If they stayed in a state of near constant darkness after several generations it would make sense that their eyes would become larger and more sensitive to the light. The man spoke.

Man: "My name is irrelevant. Congratulations, you are the first to make it this far. I shall take you to see Phoenix." Connway was seized by the other robed men. He saw the metallic glint of some kind of medical device. He felt numbness in his left arm as an osmosis tranquilizer permeated his skin. He felt very sleepy as the world closed in around him.

When Connway roused, he saw he was being tended to by some type of doctor with really big eyes. Connway guessed that they must have given him the antidote to the sleep agent. The doctor moved off and Connway was helped to his feet by two other robe clad figures. The figures took up positions behind him, almost like guards. He found himself standing before another man sitting in a large ornately decorated chair. Connway shook his head in an attempt to shrug off the sleepiness while saying, "You must be Phoenix?"

Phoenix: "They tell me you figured out a way to get by the outer defense guns."

Connway: "Oh yea, sorry about the damage."

Phoenix: "That's alright. The Starblazers didn't try that hard before."

Connway: "Before?"

Phoenix: "Oh, a few years ago they were also curious about the food gardens, but they decided that knowing where the food went was more trouble than it was worth."

Connway: "Just who are you people anyway?"

Phoenix: "We are the original Callistonian colonists."

Connway: "But I thought that you were all killed by a plague!"

Phoenix: "That is exactly what you were all supposed to think."

Connway: "Phoenix, I don't understand, why would you fake a plague?"

Phoenix: "Well we must have something to hide, I guess." A brimming smile crept across his face!

Connway: "Wait a minute. What could be so damned important that the entire population of the planet would participate in such a ruse?"

Phoenix: "All in due time my boy. Now we are aware that the Starblazers recently acquired a destroyer class vessel. I believe you call it the Osiris. Tell me how are the repairs going?"

Connway: "Just fine. How did you know about the Osiris?"

Phoenix: "Aaaaaahhh, well you see about three years ago when the Starblazers first arrived here we thought they were just simple scavengers. So we sent out a few patrols and opened fire on them. It was not until later that the pirates hooked their ships computer into one of the planet's computer main frames. The pirates were trying to find a suitable location to establish a secret base. What they didn't know was that when they hooked their computers to ours is that it acted like a two-way cable. At that time it was decided that the Callistonian's should allow the intruders to stay. You see every time they go out and return they bring newly updated information on the current state of the galaxy. Fortunately for us, most starship computers update themselves automatically whenever they come near any planetary system or large public use data storage bank. We considered their occupation of one of our old military bases to be a small price to pay for the information services that you gentlemen have been unknowingly providing."

Connway: "Okay. I follow you so far. But why are you telling me all this if it is supposed to be such a big secret and all?"

Phoenix: "Well we went into hiding because at the time we did not have the firepower to defend ourselves."

Connway: "Oh, now I get it. You want the Osiris!"

Phoenix: "Yes."

Connway: "Well, even if I wanted to give it to you I couldn't. It is not mine."

Phoenix: "Whose is it?"

Connway: "Well that is a good question."

The two guards leaned in toward Connway in a threatening manner.

Connway: "No, no, you don't understand. You see in order to get the ship functioning I had to activate the A.I. computer. Normally this would not be a problem but I had to give him full control of everything when I stole it."

Phoenix: "When you stole it? I find it hard to believe that you stole a destroyer all by yourself."

Connway explained the entire story from start to finish about how he had to retrieve the Osiris from the debris field of a battle site. Of course as he told the story it got better until Connway was the hero and savior of the entire salvage team!

Phoenix: "So you are telling me that a computer named "Mo" has control of the ship?"

Connway: "Well not exactly. You see, he seems to listen to me, and when it suits him he seems to follow most orders of Captain Leslie."

Phoenix scratched his head in befuddlement. "So how do I convince this "Mo" to join me in defense of Callisto?"

Connway took a deep breath and let out a moaning sigh. He had no idea!

Connway had enough troubles just getting Mo to listen to him half the time. Not to mention Captain Leslie and now this Phoenix guy.

Connway: "I am curious by the way. Why did the Callisto people move underground?"

Phoenix: "You are trying to change the subject. But I will answer your question anyway. When we faked the plague we had to make it appear as if everybody was dead. So we dug in and hid. We have complete underground food plantations and most of our power comes from above ground solar collecting turbines."

Connway: "Now that I know of your existence and that you want the Osiris what are you going to do with me?"

Phoenix: "Probably kill you."

Connway's face turned pale.

Phoenix let out a bellowing laugh and said, "Oh, I'm just kidding my friend, (still chuckling) you should have seen your face. You turned white as a ghost! Seriously though, it sounds like I am going to need your help in convincing "Mo" to join us."

Connway's face slumped again. First off he had no idea how he would go about such a task, and second he was not sure if he even wanted to help these people. After all he practically doesn't even really know anything about them. Not to mention whatever this big secret of theirs is that they seem to be hiding.

Phoenix: "From what you tell me about Mo, it sounds like he has been programmed to defend the interests of entire planets. Since Callisto is populated and needs defending, perhaps you can build on that to convince Mo to help us."

Connway was a bit relieved. If they needed help then they probably were not going to kill him.

Connway: "Well then I guess I will just be running along then, and see what Mo thinks of the whole idea."

Connway started to step backwards when he bumped into the two guards behind him. With a slight cringe he managed to keep himself from turning and acknowledging his blunder. Phoenix waved his hand and Connway felt that cold injection of another shot of sleep agent.

CHAPTER TEN

Released

Upon awakening Connway found himself on the cold steel floor of the entrance that he came in. The two laser defense turrets were now black and lifeless. As he rolled over to pick himself up he felt a pain in his left side. As he pulled up his shirt he discovered a small mark along the underside of his left rib. It was not a scratch, it was definitely an incision. Connway poked at it and could definitely feel something beneath the skin. He was guessing that since the Callistonian's let him go they must have implanted him with some sort of tracking device. He would have to get that taken care of.

Connway made his way back to the upper levels of the planet. Once he had returned to the Starblazers base he was informed that they had been looking for him for several hours now and demanded to know where he had wandered off to? Connway would only tell them that he needed some time alone to think and that he required a shuttle to the Osiris.

As Connway came aboard the Osiris, Mo gleefully greeted him. Before Connway even got across the landing bay he was queried by Curly. "Advisor Connway, where are my security bots?" Connway paused, he had so much on his mind right now he had totally forgotten about the bots. He had to think quickly, very quickly! "Um, Curly … I have some good news and some bad news. The good news is that your security bots did an outstanding job. They fought bravely against incredible odds and laid down their lives to protect me! The bad news is that they were both destroyed in the conflict." There was a long silence. Finally Connway spoke.,"Curly, is everything ok?"

Curly: "I was rather looking forward to their return."

Connway: "I am sorry Curly. There was nothing I could do."

Curly: "Did you find the parts I require?"

Connway was thinking as fast as he could. His brain was scrambling for ideas! "As a matter of fact I met some friends who may be willing to supply you with parts if you are willing to help them out in return."

Curly: "What do they need?"

Connway suddenly realized that he was still standing in the middle of the landing bay. There were several crewmembers about that were unloading additional supplies.

Connway: "We should talk about this in private."

Connway made his way towards his quarters. On his way he was interrupted yet again. Capt. Leslie had spotted him in the corridor and was chasing after him.

Capt. Leslie: "Connway! Where the hell have you been? I want to know if you have made any progress on what we talked about before?" She made a subtle gesture toward the ship indicating the A.I.'s may be listening.

Connway was visibly showing signs of discomfort and gritted his teeth while saying, "I'm working on it."

Connway hastily departed the Captain and proceeded to his quarters. He was just walking in the door when Curly asked, "What was that woman talking about?"

Connway: "Woman? Oh, you mean Capt. Leslie."

Connway was taken by a realization. Curly did not recognize Leslie as the Captain! Connway's stomach sank. This was not a good thing!

Connway: "Um, the woman wants me to take care of some things for her."

Curly: "Well, tell her you are busy. Now what do these friends of ours need in trade for parts?"

Connway was overjoyed to hear Curly use the word "ours". It was the first time that he had made any indication that he may be willing to work with them.

Connway: "Well, these friends are called Callistonians and they want us to help protect their planet."

Just then "Mo chimed in, "Where did they come from and why should we protect their interests?"

Connway was startled! He hadn't realized that Mo had been listening in the whole time. It then occurred to him that both Mo and Curly were using the same network of sensors throughout the ship and that anything that one discussed was sure to be heard by the other. Connway had once entertained the idea of having Mo help shut down Curly, but now that would prove to be impossible since he would not be able to talk to Mo in private.

Curly: "That is a good question. According to the database Callisto is supposed to be a dead planet."

Connway: "Yea, uh ... well apparently the whole plague thing was a ruse. They have been hiding down there for decades!"

Mo began scanning the records of the database. He was looking for any information that would tell him if Callisto was the sovereign property of Venus or possibly a rebelling territory. Unfortunately his on board records did not go back that far. The only data he had was that it was a plague planet and was to be avoided.

Curly on the other hand had been tasked with ship security and did not care where or how he got his resources and supplies. Curly was also scanning records. Only he was looking for manufacturing capabilities and resources of the planet. Curly was disappointed in that the records were incomplete.

Mo and Curly together: "Why have they been hiding?"

A shudder went down Connway's spine. The two computers were using different tones of voice so that one could easily tell them apart when speaking with the A.I.'s but now they both had the same question and were speaking simultaneously, the combination of their voices together was powerful and eerie at the same time. To further complicate the matter that was the one question that he had not been able to get an answer on from Phoenix.

Connway: "I am not certain why they have been hiding. Although I get the impression that they are protecting something. I am not sure what it is yet, but it must be pretty important if the whole planet is in on it."

Mo: "I need more information."

Curly: "I concur."

Connway felt relieved. He was not quite sure why. He just did. Perhaps it had something to do with being grilled with questions from two artificially intelligent computers. He had never really been in a situation like that before, especially since he could not answer all of their questions. Connway decided to go up to the bridge. He had not shown up for work in a few days and felt he should at least make an appearance.

When he arrived on the bridge he was pleasantly surprised to see Michele there. She was lying under her computer station and appeared to be working on it. This puzzled him since the terminal looked like it was operating just fine. She looked up from her efforts and smiled. Connway nodded and proceeded over to another terminal. As he crossed the bridge he caught a glimpse out the forward observation window. The Osiris was surrounded by the old gantry work of the decaying orbital shipyard. There were several people in spacesuits jetting around making repairs and even a couple of space capable repair bots floating about. As he checked his computer station he found several progress reports that had been sent to him by the repair teams over the last few days. According to the reports repairs were nearly complete now and they just about had a fully functional destroyer class warship!

Capt. Leslie entered the bridge. Upon her arrival Michele and several other crew members stood at attention and were just about to salute when Leslie raised her hand to stop them and waved them off. It was just then that Capt. Leslie noticed that Connway had not stood up to greet her. Connway seemed to be completely engrossed in his work. She proceeded over to his station and looked over his shoulder to see what could be so interesting.

It appeared that Connway was trying to dig up information on the old plague that had wiped out the Callistonians. Capt. Leslie was most curious, "What are you looking that up for?" Connway was caught off guard. He hadn't noticed the Captain coming in and sneaking up on him. Connway explained that he had had an encounter with a Callistonian. There was a long pause. The bridge crew seemed to be taken aback. Connway went on to explain that they had taken him hostage and that they were highly organized and their objective is to acquire the Osiris. At first Capt. Leslie was hesitant to believe his story, but when Connway lifted his shirt to show her the incision just under his rib she really began to worry.

Leslie, Michele, and Connway went to the infirmary to have his scar checked out. As the threesome entered the infirmary they saw a modest sized room with very modern looking equipment, scanners, and probes. A medical technician turned to greet them and asked how she could assist them.

Capt. Leslie explained that they wanted to have a closer look at the incision by Connway's rib. The attractive blonde med. tech instructed Connway to remove his shirt and lay on the examining table. As Connway made himself comfortable Michele moved around the table and grasped his hand. Connway looked up into Michele's big brown eyes and smiled. Leslie on the other hand had a scowl on her face. She was very possessive of Michele and didn't like to see her with anybody else. The med. tech slid on a large glove like device that was covered with all kinds of micro sensors and wires. As she moved the gloved hand over Connway's chest a computer screen on the wall automatically lit up displaying his heart rate, blood pressure, and body temperature. The tech then used her other hand to make several adjustments on the glove and soon the display screen was showing an X-ray of his ribs. She began to slowly move down his ribcage and the scanner displayed what appeared to be a wire and a small circuit board looking device. The tech raised an eyebrow and said, "What the hell is that?"

Capt. Leslie: "That is what we came to ask you."

Med. tech: "Um … well. It is a foreign object located in his body."

Connway: "No shit!"

Michele: "Yea, but what does it do?"

The med. tech continued to examine the device. She determined that it was not connected to or influencing any bodily functions and that it appeared to also have its own micro battery for a power source. After spending some time with the ship's data base and comparing the scan of the device she finally announced that it was a transmitter. A location device used to track the whereabouts of a given person.

Connway: "Can you remove it?"

Med. tech: "Of course!"

Capt. Leslie: "Hold on a minute, can we use this thing to our advantage? Can we track them with it?"

Connway was not sure he liked the sound of all this. He just wanted the damn thing out of his gut. The med tech went back to scanning his ribcage. She now had a much better idea of what she was looking at. After a few more moments she informed them that it was monitoring his heart beat and that if they removed it whoever was tracking him would know that it had either been removed or that he was dead. Connway secretly preferred the removed option.

Capt. Leslie instructed them to leave the device where it was for now. She wanted to think about how she could use this. She was a wonderful opportunist in that way. The threesome left the infirmary and went back to the bridge.

Philip had been spending all his time in engineering. With the help of the space bots he had just about managed to get the ship completely repaired. Thinking of the space bots it occurred to Philip that Capt. Leslie had ordered the crew to try and track all the robot drones. The crew was having moderate success in tagging the drones aboard the ship, but nobody attempted to follow the space bots. It then occurred to him that the space bots must dock somewhere and it should be a simple matter to just follow one of them and it should lead him right to that secret manufacturing plant! Philip was just about to put on the helmet to his spacesuit when one of his technical engineers came up to him.

Tech: "Sir, I just heard you got your Starblazer emblem laser etching. Congratulations Sir!"

Philip let a smile creep across his face and shook the man's outstretched hand.

Philip: "Oh, by the way, I am going outside to follow on of the space bots. Help me put on one of these thruster packs."

Philip decided to use a manual air-lock escape hatch. If he were to use an automated air-lock door then the A.I.'s would know he was outside. This way he could possibly sneak up on one of the space bots undetected. He unscrewed the locking mechanism on the escape hatch with his foot. Then he began the manual depressurization sequence. Once all the air was gone he unlocked the outer door. Philip looked out into the blackness of space. He took a deep breath and said to himself, "The first step is always a doozy!" Philip fired the rocket pack and launched himself out into the great unknown.

As he glided through space the massive rusted girders of the orbital space station came into view. The girders were almost majestic in their strength and aged form. Philip was a man who could appreciate quality work. He fired his maneuver thrusters and he began to make his way towards the port side of the Osiris. It was not long before he spotted one of the disc shaped space bots finishing up on the outer hull. As the bot moved off Philip discretely followed from a moderate distance behind. The bot went down to the cargo bay and retrieved another piece of metal. Philip was expecting the bot to return to the same location that it had been working on. Only this time it moved upward and over the artificial horizon created by the Osiris. Philip quickly scrambled to catch up. As he crested the upper curve of the Osiris he saw the space bot delivering the piece of metal to a portion of the Osiris which appeared to be completely undamaged. Upon watching what happened next he saw the plate of steel being welded directly to the outside hull of the Osiris in a vertical position. Philip decided he wanted a closer look at this. He waited patiently for the bot to complete its work and move off.

After it was clear, Philip thrusted over for a look. It appeared that there was an entire section being grafted into place. Philip started to skirt the perimeter of it to see if he could get an idea of just how big it really was, as his feet glided just a few inches above the outer hull to the new wall plating on his right side. It was just over the height of a man and well-constructed. There was a light coming from ahead. Philip paused, he thought it might be another space bot. Philip did not want to be discovered but there was no place to hide. He waited. The light did not appear to be moving. Philip found this to be curious as well. Moving forward again, he proceeded with extreme caution. It turned out that the light was coming from a porthole in the wall. This was perfect, for now he could see what was inside! As Philip drifted up to the window he peered in and saw a full scale manufacturing plant completely run by robots.

There was no gravity in the plant. A robot on one side of the factory literally threw a circuit board across the bay and it glided over to another bot which caught it. The second bot then placed it into yet another bot that it was building and soldered it in place. As one looked around the room you could see various parts floating here and there. There were bits of wire, gears, optical lenses, wheels and all manner of things. Philip was amazed at the efficiency of the whole thing. At this rate of production he postulated that Curly must have many more bots than anyone thought!

While Philip was busy watching the automated bots assemble even more bots, a small spherical bot about 10 inches in diameter glided up to the window. Philip pushed back from the window as the little unit turned and shined a mini spot light on him! The light sensitive visor plate on Philip's spacesuit immediately darkened from the sudden illumination. Philip however knew that he was busted! The little bot disappeared from sight. Philip was almost panicky! He started to make his way back towards the air-lock escape hatch that he came out of.

Curly immediately dispatched his space bots to take care of the spy who had discovered his secret hide out. Philip saw a space bot round the way and could tell it was coming straight for him. To his astonishment Philip was amazed at the graceful maneuverability of the approaching bot. Unfortunately, this was working against him! Philip engaged his thruster pack and was going to try and out distance it. It was a slow motion race. In space you had to move gently and lightly or you would careen off course into oblivion. Philip guided his way to the escape hatch. He had forgotten that he had left the hatch open when he left. Only now he was extremely glad that he had. As he raced for the hatch he angled himself like a torpedo and charged head first for the tiny opening. He knew that he was traveling much to fast but he figured he would stop himself with his hands when he hit the inner hatch. Philip took a deep breath and hoped he was going to hit the hole just right. As he surged into the escape tube he let go his breath with a sigh of relief, he had made his mark and quickly threw up his hands to stop his forward acceleration. Philip stopped with a sudden thud as he hit the inner hatch with considerable force. He was banged up, but no worse for the trip. As he peered downward he could now see the sleek space bot pivoting around in pursuit. Philip reached out with his right foot and hooked the inner handle of the outer escape hatch. The hatch slammed shut with a clang! Philip pushed his foot into the spokes of the locking handle for the hatch and fired his thruster pack. Philip began to spin sideways in violent turning action. As he spun his foot rotated the locking handle and spun the hatch shut.

Philip put his hands out and dragged them against the wall of the escape tube. After several more revolutions he managed to bring himself to a stop. Taking a moment to collect his senses Philip could now hear a crackling and the inside of the tube lit up with a bright bluish light. Looking down he saw that the space bot outside was using its laser cutter to burn its way in! It was still coming after him! With the incision punctured in the outer hatch Philip knew he would be unable to pressurize the tube and open the inner hatch. He knew he was in trouble! Philip clicked on the radio in his helmet.

Philip: "Mayday! Mayday! I am under attack! I found the robot manufacturing plant. It is on top of the Osiris on the outside of the ship!"

Curly activated a radio jammer. All communications in the area went hazy. The space bot had now managed to cut the hinge pins on the outer escape hatch and its claws grabbed and crunched into the metal. Philip looked just in time to see the hatch being torn away and chucked into outer space. The bot reached in and its claw crushed down on Philip's right ankle! Philip screamed in agony but no one could hear him. As the bot backed up it dragged Philip yelling and clawing at the inside of the escape tube. There was no way he could escape from the mechanical clutches of the bot.

Philip was hyperventilating now. It dawned on him that if he kept struggling that he might tear his spacesuit. Philip tried to calm himself. He adjusted his air supply. He made it oxygen rich. It was much easier to breath now. Philip was slowly regaining his sense of control.

On the bridge of the Osiris Michele looked at Capt. Leslie. They had just received the radio call telling them that the robot manufacturing plant was on the top of the ship. Only they had lost radio contact with whoever sent the message. They were running a systems check to try and figure out why they had lost communications. Connway pivoted around in his chair to face Capt. Leslie. He called out to the air.

Connway: "Mo, what's wrong with radio communications?

Mo: "Nothing. All circuits are functioning normally."

Connway: "Are we being jammed?"

Capt. Leslie's face turned pale with stark realization.

Mo: "Yes."

Connway: "What is the source of the jamming signal?"

Mo: "Curly."

Captain Leslie: "Son of a bitch!"

Michele: "The voice sounded like Philip. Mo, where is Philip?"

Mo: "Scanning."

Mo: "I do not detect Philip on board the Osiris."

Connway: "Try scanning outside the ship."

Mo: "Unidentified personnel off the lower port side."

Capt. Leslie: "Show me."

The cameras on the port side had been replaced by now and Mo put up the image on the main observation screen at the front of the bridge. The command crew looked on as they saw a space bot dragging off a man in a spacesuit by his ankle. The man appeared to be trying to use his thruster pack to fight back and pull in the opposite direction. The crew watched helplessly as they observed the space bot ignite its cutting torch!

Upon seeing the cutting torch light up Philip remembered that he had an oxygen rich mix in his suit! He desperately attempted to adjust his air. The space bot swung the torch over onto the captured ankle. It quickly burned its way through the spacesuit and the intense flames entered the oxygen rich interior. The flames flashed up inside of the suit gathering intensity as they went!

From the bridge Michele cupped her hands over her face. Connway's mouth dropped open, and Leslie's eyes were wide with horror. Philip's spacesuit exploded in a fiery ball of flames!

The space bot tumbled back in the opposite direction. The bot tried to fire its stabilizer thrusters to compensate for the spinning action. As the bridge crew tracked the wayward bot they saw it smash into one of the huge girders that made up the Calisto repair station. The bot flew apart into a million pieces!

Curly was upset. First his secret manufacturing plant had been discovered, and second he had not planned on losing one of his space bots!

Capt. Leslie clicked on the internal address system inside the Osiris.

Capt. Leslie: "All hands battle station! I am declaring the A.I. Curly to be hostile. The secret manufacturing plant is located on the top exterior of the ship."

The Captain's speech was interrupted by the sound of static. Curly had cut off her broadcast in mid-sentence. Mo had a choice to make. He could either side with Curly, a fellow A.I. or with the humans. Mo spent several milliseconds pondering his decision. After much consideration he arrived at the fact that Curly had just killed a crewmember of the Osiris. Mo decided that Curly had lost sight of who the enemy was. Although Mo was not currently sure of that himself, he did recognize his own crew and what Curly did was wrong. Mo attempted to re-engage the intercom system.

Curly however countered with a power surge to trip the circuit breakers to the intercom system effectively rendering it inoperative for the time being.

CHAPTER
ELEVEN

End Game

Mo and Curly had now officially gone to war with each other! The first thing Mo did was to gain positive control of the environmental systems. That way he could protect his human crew from depressurization. Meanwhile Curly went after power systems. He was ensuring that he would not be shut down. Mo shunted control of the internal cameras and sensors to himself while Curly managed to secure external sensors.

On board the bridge Capt. Leslie observed the main computer screen. It was displaying which systems were being taken over by the two different A.I.'s. She quickly realized that they had to act fast and that no ship's system could at present be depended on. She grabbed her belt and pulled out her personnel communications link. She began barking orders to her crew one crew member at a time.

Meanwhile the A.I.'s were heavily engaged in a most lethal game of cyber war! They each had their own security passwords as well as code cracking programs. Since they were both programmed with the same computer software they both began rotating password systems and each had the same chance of defeating the other for control of the Osiris. The real variables were going to be the humans versus the bots.

Three crewmembers of the Starblazer rushed up to the top decks of the Osiris. They were promptly met by security bots. A hellish battle ensued. Laser bolts were impacting all down the corridor in both directions! The hall had begun to fill with smoke from the burning metal. Neither side seemed to be making any headway until one of the young humans fell back and ran down the hall. The remaining two turned to call their comrade a coward when the security bot switched over to infrared sights and gunned down the humans. As it turned out the third human was not running at all. He had reached a weapons closet around the corner and was scooping up several anti-personnel grenades! The poor lad heard the death screams of his compatriots and knew there was nothing he could do. He peered back around the corner and angrily hurled a grenade! There was a deafening explosion after the smoke cleared the young man saw the bot laid in pieces. Although there was a terrible ringing in the boy's ears he took a moment of satisfaction in his accomplishment. Slowly his smile disappeared as he saw the door to the manufacturing plant slide open and another security bot replaced the destroyed one. This bot moved slower than the last one, but it appeared to have heavier armor. The young man chose wisdom above bravado and beat a hasty retreat!

Connway nearly fell out of his seat from the violent rattling of the ship. He exclaimed, "What the hell was that?"

Capt. Leslie: "That would be the sound of a grenade going off!"

Michele: "Not good, not good at all!"

Michele was reaching under the lip of her computer console. She came up with a large intimidating looking laser rifle! It had an over/under configuration, with a forward pistol grip mount. Michele looked over at Connway and shrugged while saying, "Well, a girls got to be prepared for anything these days." She smiled, inserted an energy clip and marched off the bridge!

Down by engineering the technicians could hear laser fire down the hall from the room they were working in. Several of the young men thrust open an emergency weapons cabinet and passed out laser guns. The men very carefully opened the door to the room and were just about to look outside when one tech held up a wrench and motioned the other to wait a moment. He silently threw the wrench out the door. Before the wrench even hit the floor there was a flash of bright red light that lit up the hall as the double barreled guns from a security bot vaporized the wrench in midair. The technicians looked at each other with a sense of awe!

It was not difficult for the techs to figure that there was a bot stationed just outside the door waiting for them to come out. As the men discussed it for a moment they figured that it would take the bot about ¾ of a second to lock onto and target an individual. If one of them were to jump out the door and start firing immediately, then they figured they had a chance of taking down the bot first. A brave soul by the name of Thor stepped forward. He was originally from Earth, St. Thomas, Jamaica and he hated bots! He was 12 years old when he tried to steal his first hover car, and it was a police bot that busted him. Thor felt this would be the perfect opportunity to settle a grudge.

Another tech was peering out the doorway and said that he could see laser score marks on the floor. Judging by the direction of the burns he figured that the bot must be on the left side of the door down the hall somewhere. Thor plucked the laser pistol from the hand of another tech. Now that he had one in each hand he was ready for battle. Thor stood next to the doorway. He took a deep breath and rushed out with both guns blazing! As he turned left he unleashed a horrendous volley of searing energy down the hall. Thor had aimed about three feet off the floor. He knew bots were short. With stark realization he discovered that the hall was empty! Thor heard movement. As he turned to see where it came from he was mortified to discover that the bot was hovering along the ceiling. The last thing he saw was the red gun barrels of the bot shooting him right in the chest!

The other technicians in engineering saw Thor get blown backward as he fell to the ground. The laser pistol in his left hand skidded back and lay motionless on the floor. One of the techs saw that Thor's right hand was right by the doorway and chanced reaching to grab him. With a quick heave he was able to pull Thor's still body back in the room. The young men looked pale. Sure they were cutthroat pirates and all, but this enemy had no emotion and could patiently wait them out forever. The tech looked down at the entry wound in Thor's chest. It was high and in the middle. Another man flipped the body over and they saw the exit burn in his lower back. The men hadn't anticipated a high angle attack. The robotic opponents were very clever as well.

One of the technicians used his communicator to contact the bridge.

Tech: "Captain we are in engineering and we are pinned down by a bot in the hallway. The damn bot is on the ceiling!"

Michele overheard the transmission and clicked in, "I'm on it! I'll be there in 5 minutes."

Michele was staying close to the walls. Whenever she got to a turn in the hallway she took out her compact. Using her make up mirror she would look around the corner and make sure there were no bots waiting to ambush someone. She managed to make her way to the hall where the engineers were pinned down. Being sure to check the ceilings she tilted her mirror upward and sure enough, there was a security bot comfortably hanging upside down on the ceiling in the middle of the hall. Michele wondered why it hadn't taken a pot shot at the mirror. Either the bot was using infrared rather than motion detectors, or it was only targeting larger objects. She watched the bot for a few moments. It seemed to be occupied with scanning in both directions down the corridor. Michele had an idea. She used her radio to call the technicians in the engine room. She told one of them to quickly stick his hand out into the hall. The object was to leave his hand exposed just long enough for the bot to target it but pull it back in before it had a chance to fire. She would use this as a diversion in order to get a clean shot from her position. The remaining engineers nominated the new guy to do it. He was a young kid that had only recently become a Starblazer. He was not happy about his nomination but the others out ranked him and convinced him that he had to follow orders.

Michele radioed that she was ready. They would coordinate their efforts on the count of three. As she counted, the new guy stuck his hand out the door and flipped off the bot. The bot spun around and the new guy pulled his hand back just as a searing bolt of raw energy erupted past the doorway. Seizing her chance, Michele quickly popped out from her position at the other end of the hall and raised her rifle skyward. There was a terrible sound of thunder as she hit her mark and the bot thudded off the ceiling. The bot fell to the floor with a crash! The engineers let out a victory cheer. As they poured out into the hall to congratulate her, Michele moved up keeping her gun trained on the bot. The new guy engineer ran up to the bot and gave it a swift kick saying, "Yea, take that you pile of junk!" Michele shouldered her rifle as the rest of the engineers shook their heads. Fortunately the bot was indeed dead, but the more experienced engineers knew to always double check those things that just tried to kill you.

Sgt. Tiberious emerged from slip stream and was bringing the Starblazer around the way towards Calisto I space station. They had sustained an unusual amount of damage for such a brief encounter. Of course they didn't normally face off with hardened military forces either. Still, he was not looking forward to telling Capt. Leslie that he just got his ass handed to him.

Curly had an idea. He was going to get the humans to leave the Osiris voluntarily. He purposely sent false data to the reactor room! He was making it look like there was a radiation leak. After a few moments Curly noticed that the crew did not appear to even notice that the reactors were appearing to overload. Then Curly remembered that the ship wide address system was not in working order. Consequently the automated voice warning system could not be heard. The crew would have normally noticed the gauges that were red lining, but with all the commotion going on with the skirmishes with the bots, no one was watching their screens. Curly had to come up with a way to draw the humans' attention to the computer screens in such a way as to not tip his hand in his deception.

The cute blonde on the Starblazer informed Sgt. Tiberious that for some reason she could not raise the Osiris on the radio. Sgt. Tiberious thought this to be most unusual. The Sgt. got out his personnel communicator and would call Capt. Leslie directly. The only problem was that it was a small unit and had limited broadcast range. He gave orders for them to take the Starblazer closer to the Osiris.

Curly had figured it out. He would set fire to something! The fire alarm was completely separate from the address system and even had its own backup power supply. Curly located a nice flammable little couch and had one of the security bots light it up with a short burst of laser fire. As the smoke from the couch filled one of the empty rooms in the housing quarters section of the ship the alarm claxons sang out their song of discord!

After closing the distance Sgt. Tiberious radioed Capt. Leslie. He was about to give a report status of his mission when he was cut off by her voice shouting to overcome the sound of fire alarms and laser fire in the background.

Capt. Leslie: "Boy, am I glad to see you! Get over here with the Starblazer and pull up to the air lock with the missing escape pod on the bridge!"

Sgt. Tiberious: "What the hell is going on over there?"

Capt. Leslie: "Now Sgt. Get over here now!"

Sgt. Tiberious moved across his own bridge and pushed aside the pilot. They were going to have to take the Starblazer in between the Orbital repair station's girder work, and the Osiris. It was going to be a tight fit but the Sgt. was an excellent pilot back in his day and he wasn't going to let an inexperienced rookie fly his ship into a girder.

Capt. Leslie was using her communicator to relay orders to abandon ship! The A.I.'s were having a full blown cyber war. The bots were gunning down crew and it looked like one of the reactors had caught fire! They were gonna lose it!

Most of the crew of the Osiris was able to get to the rear launch bay unmolested. It was rather convenient that Curly had cleared a path for them to escape. Curly was almost smug with satisfaction.

Sgt. Tiberious realized that the Starblazer would not physically fit in between the girders and the Osiris. However the great thing about space was that it was relative. He fired the Starblazer's maneuver thrusters and rotated his craft 90 degrees. He very gingerly edged forward to slip into his new parking space. The crew on the bridge of the Starblazer looked out of one of the portholes as one of the station's girders passed by within inches. The all-female crew was both impressed and a little nervous at the same time.

Curly observed the Starblazer moving closer and launched his last space bot.

As the Sgt. got into position he radioed over to the Capt. saying, "Did anybody call a taxi?"

Capt. Leslie: "Just open your airlock doors and give us a minute."

Connway was busy breaking out a couple of spacesuits from a nearby gear locker. Since the escape pod on the bridge was missing they would have to cross the space between the Osiris and the Starblazer the hard way.

As Capt. Leslie was putting on her spacesuit she was interrupted by yet another call from the Sgt. "Hey, do you know anything about a space bot? I got one coming right for us on a collision course."

Capt. Leslie: "Destroy it! Blow it out of the air right now!"

Sgt. Tiberious was not entirely sure what was going on but his gunners loved to shoot things anyway! Before he even finished giving the order the starboard side cannon came alive with intensity. The space bot went up like a beautiful fireworks display on the Fourth of July!

Connway and the Capt. cycled through the air-lock on the Osiris. They could see the open hatch of the Starblazer waiting for them just across the way. With a gentle push they both started to cross over to their waiting salvation. During the brief excursion into space they could see several ships leaving the rear cargo bay. Capt. Leslie was relieved to see that her people were safely away. As they entered the Starblazer air-lock doors slid shut behind them.

Connway turned around in the Starblazer's airlock and looked back out the window at the Osiris. It was moving.

Connway: "Hey, whose flying?"

Capt. Leslie turned to look out the window. "What the Hell?"

Curly had another brainstorm. Why was he wasting time in a cyber-war with Mo? He would attack him directly in the physical world. Curly sent one of his bots to Mo's central processing core, data crystal storage room. Curly ordered his bot to start removing crystals directly from Mo's central processor!

Mo began to feel impotent. He was losing his senses. As he dulled down he finally realized what Curly was doing. A direct attack. The only problem was Mo had no bots! He was helpless to defend himself. It only took a few more moments and Curly got complete control of the Osiris.

As the Starblazer repositioned itself within the Callisto I station they observed the Osiris orbiting Calisto. They even tracked a transmission between the Osiris and the planet's surface but they were unable to decipher what it was. The crew on the Starblazer began making repairs of the damages that had been incurred during their brush with the I.A.F.

The following day Capt. Leslie was sitting in the command chair of the Starblazer when their radar screens lit up like a firestorm. There were hundreds of ships lifting off from the surface of the planet/moon. Connway knew that these forces had to belong to Phoenix, but there were so many of them! The ships were on a trajectory towards the Osiris. Even though the Osiris was a destroyer class vessel if it were to be attacked by that many ships it would surely lose the fight. The Osiris however was not moving off. In fact she was opening her aft cargo doors!

Connway remembered what Phoenix had done to him and put his hand by his left rib.

Connway: "Hey wait a minute, what radio frequency was the Osiris using when it broadcast to the planet yesterday?"

A technician gave him the frequency and Capt. Leslie immediately recognized it as the same as the tracking device that Connway had.

Capt. Leslie: "That son of a bitch! Curly sold us out to the Callistonians!"

They watched as the Phoenix fleet gathered around the Osiris in a combat formation with the Osiris at the lead command position. Two smaller Phoenix ships were proceeding to dock with the Osiris. One of them looked like some sort of transport and the other was around front near the torpedo tubes. As they watched the space ballet Leslie observed the transfer of torpedo after torpedo to the Osiris. Phoenix was obviously planning something big.

Now that they realized what frequency they were operating on Connway instructed the communications technician to establish a new link to the Osiris. As the bridge cameras came into focus Connway saw Phoenix sitting in the command chair of Osiris. Phoenix looked up at his screen and was delighted to see Connway.

Phoenix: "Connway my boy! How are you?"

Connway: "Not as good as you. You seem to have an awful lot of ships there. Planning on going somewhere?"

Phoenix: "As a matter of fact we are. You see we decided that in order to ensure our autonomy it would be a prudent move to strike first. In just a couple hours our new friend Curly is going to help us hit Earth."

Connway: "By the way. Now that you have come out, would you mind telling me why you people faked a plague and all?"

Phoenix: "Immortality my friend, immortality. You see I am 800 years old. About 700 years ago the colonists on Callisto noticed that nobody was dying. At least not of old age anyway. That's when the scientists figured out that due to the magnetic field that surrounds Jupiter, and reaches over Callisto, that together they seem to preserve the human genome for longevity. You see if we were to make it public that Callisto offered everlasting life, well you can see that we would have been overrun."

Connway: "So in order to keep it secret you concocted a story about a plague in order to give you enough time to build a defensive force of your own!"

Phoenix: "Exactly. We were just about ready to announce our presence here when we discovered you guys were going after a destroyer class vessel. We just couldn't pass that up. With the help of Curly here we should have a definite advantage in battle!"

Connway: "But you will kill millions in your attack on Earth."

Phoenix: "So."

Connway was born on Venus and could really care less about Earth. He just didn't want to see all those people get killed. He surmised that the Callistonians felt that Callisto was their home and also did not care about Earth. He would have to try a new approach.

Connway: "But you guys have been alive for 800 years. If you go to war you might be killed."

Phoenix: "That would be a good thing. You see some of us are actually getting tired of living! Besides, we are still having children and we are beginning to get an overcrowding situation as well as some minor food shortages on Callisto. You see we have no choice but to go to war!"

Connway had no argument for that. What Phoenix was saying actually made sense. Callisto had to go to war. It would solve half of their problems in one fell swoop!

Capt. Leslie lowered her head and groaned, "I am tired of all this. Let's go to Mars!"

THE
END

A S A   P u b l i s h i n g   C o m p a n y

33282277R00092

Made in the USA
Charleston, SC
09 September 2014